Moon Over The Mountains

by

Donna Baker

Dales Large Print Books
Long Preston, North Yorkshire,
BD23 4ND, England.

British Library Cataloguing in Publication Data.

Baker, Donna
    Moon over the mountains.

    A catalogue record of this book is
    available from the British Library

    ISBN   1-84262-085-1 pbk

First published in Great Britain 1977 by Robert Hale Limited

Copyright © Donna Baker 1977

Cover illustration © John Hancock by arrangement with
P.W.A. International Ltd.

The moral right of the author has been asserted

Published in Large Print 2001 by arrangement with
Caroline Sheldon

Dales Large Print is an imprint of Library Magna Books Ltd.

Printed and bound in Great Britain by
T.J. (International) Ltd., Cornwall, PL28 8RW

MOON OVER
THE MOUNTAINS

ONE

'Will passengers for Flight 17 to Amsterdam please…' The announcer's voice was lost in a sudden hubbub of crockery and spoons. Tracy Pelham, turning from the counter to take her coffee back to the seat at the other side of the airport lounge, checked abruptly to avoid knocking into a woman with a baby – and felt a sharp nudge from behind.

'What on earth are you doing? Why can't you look where you're going? Why stop just there?' a furious voice demanded, and Tracy turned quickly. A tall, powerfully built man stood glowering at her and mopping at some spots of coffee on his otherwise immaculate grey suit. 'I was just behind you when you stopped so suddenly,' he continued, 'Look at this – coffee everywhere. Daft, dithering females!'

'I'm not a dithering female!' Tracy exclaimed indignantly, and then stopped. Why should she explain to this arrogant man, anyway? 'You shouldn't have been so close.' She held out her hand. 'Shall I hold your

7

cup while you mop up?'

'No, thank you! I don't want to be drowned in the stuff.' He glanced coldly at her, his eyes the blue of Arctic ice under dark lowering brows. His hair was thick, almost black, and Tracy found herself, absurdly contrasting its extreme darkness with the white-blonde of her own short curls. She shook herself mentally – what difference did it make to her what colour his hair was? They had met, momentarily, in a crowded airport lounge, and were never likely to meet again. At least – glancing again at those steely blue eyes under the dark scowling brows – she hoped not!

'I'm sorry about your suit,' she said stiffly, although he seemed to have got most of the spots out by now. 'I really couldn't help it.' And she turned away and made her way over to the seat where she had left her luggage.

The departure lounge was crowded on this May Saturday, although Tracy supposed that it was probably not nearly so bad as it would be later in the season. There were still two or three vacant places on the comfortable seats in the corner she had chosen, although several people had arrived and taken positions while she was away buying her coffee. She lowered the cup to the table and sat down, thankful for the chance of a breather in the hurried morning, and caught the eye of a young man sitting opposite.

He was a pleasant-looking fellow, she thought, quite different from the frowning Scot she had just left – it was only now that she identified the slight burr in his voice. Impatiently, she pushed the memory of him out of her mind – he was no more than a small irritation in an otherwise blue sky – and, responding to the friendly glance of the brown eyes opposite her, smiled tentatively.

'I see we're heading for the same destination,' the young man remarked, nodding at her luggage. Tracy glanced down at it, and then at his own suitcases; sure enough, the same green labels adorned them both, with the name LJUBLJANA printed in bold capitals.

'You're going to Yugoslavia too?' she said, 'Have you been before?'

'Never. Been to Austria, of course, and Switzerland. You'll find the part we're going to – Slovenia – is quite similar to Austria in many ways. Alpine meadows, snowy mountains and all that. You like that sort of scenery?'

'I'm sure I will. The pictures in the brochures looked beautiful. I've never been to Austria either, so it will all be quite new to me.'

'Well, you may get a chance to go there.' He got up and came across the small space to sit beside her. 'We'll be quite near the Austrian border, you know. And the Italian, of course. Do you know Italy?'

'I've never been abroad before at all,' Tracy confessed, smiling at him. He was really quite attractive, she thought – not handsome in the usual sense perhaps, but pleasant, with merry brown eyes that matched his soft thatch of hair, and teeth that flashed very white in his tanned face. They flashed now as he grinned back at her.

'Never been abroad? Never flown before?'

'No, never.'

'And you're travelling alone? Well, we shall have to look after you, then.' He leaned a little closer and whispered confidentially, 'Are you nervous?'

'No, of course not.' Then she laughed. 'Well, just a little, perhaps. But I'm really much more excited than nervous. It's all – so new. Even this.' She looked around the airport lounge. 'I expect it's just like going by bus for you. But for me...' Her voice

10

trailed away as she found herself staring across the lounge into a pair of eyes as cold and as blue as ice. She turned back quickly. 'How long do you think we'll be here?'

'No knowing,' her companion said easily. 'Anyway, we're early yet. Let's get to know each other, since we're to be travelling companions. My name's Nick Lester.'

'Tracy Pelham.' But she spoke vaguely, her eyes drawn again to the corner where the Scotsman leaned against the wall, slowly sipping his coffee and apparently never taking his eyes from her. Tracy wished that he would look away – or that she could prevent her own eyes from constantly straying in his direction. If only their flight could be called, and she could escape that penetrating gaze! And why was he watching her at all? They had never met before, could have no possible interest in each other. All that she had done was to spill a few drops of coffee over him – and that his own fault, for following so closely behind her. Surely he couldn't have expected her to walk right into the woman with the baby...

'And where do you come from?' Tracy brought her mind back with a jerk to Nick Lester, who had apparently just finished telling her all about himself. Guiltily, she

11

blushed and said, 'I'm sorry, my mind was wandering... It's all so exciting. What did you say?'

'Just that I come from London and work as a solicitor's clerk.' His tone was slightly nettled and Tracy hastened to soothe him; after all, he had been nothing but pleasant and friendly towards her and he really was very attractive – just the kind of young man one might hope to meet on holiday... Her thoughts saddened as she recalled the reasons behind this sudden venture abroad on her own, and once again she made a deliberate effort to return to the present.

'Oh, I'm nothing very special,' she said lightly. 'Just an ordinary secretary... My home's near Hereford – I'm really a country bumpkin! Not at all interesting, I'm afraid.'

'I wouldn't say that,' Nick's eyes rested on her with obvious appreciation. 'I should say you're very interesting indeed. Whatever are the young men of Hereford doing to be letting you come away like this on your own?'

Tracy laughed. 'Why shouldn't I? This is the age of Women's Lib, you know!'

'Oh, yes, but we don't *really* believe in it, do we,' Nick said comfortably. 'All that bra-burning and campaigning for Rights. When all anyone really wants is a good old-fashioned Romance.' He glanced at her, his brown eyes dancing. 'Don't you agree, Tracy – that Romance is *really* the thing?'

Tracy hesitated, but was saved from having to answer by an announcement which cut right across their conversation. It was the call for their flight – the flight to Ljubljana, in Yugoslavia. With a suddenly thudding heart, Tracy scrambled to pick up her bags. Soon, they would be on the plane – flying above London, over the Channel and across Europe to a country she had only the haziest of ideas about. She looked desperately round the lounge, wondering if even now she could back out, abandon the idea of the holiday – and then she felt a firm hand under her elbow, and Nick's voice in her ear, 'It's okay, Tracy. There's no rush, they always call the flights early. Look, there's our plane.'

Tracy gazed out through the window and saw the plane standing on the tarmac, long and elegant. It shone white and a blue stripe ran along the side; a blue as blue as Arctic ice, as blue as a pair of cold, angry eyes...

Tracy shook herself and put down her suitcases, then she said impulsively. 'It's so much nicer to have someone to share it all with – don't you think so?'

13

The aircraft was really rather like a huge bus. A long gangway ran down the centre, with the seats in pairs on the left and threes on the right. Tracy hesitated, wondering which was the best place to sit, and felt Nick's hand push her gently from behind.

'Find a seat just in front of the wing,' he murmured. 'If you want to take photos, it gives a better perspective. That one will do. Here, give me your bag and I'll put it on the rack.'

He swung the bags up, while Tracy slid into the seat and settled herself by the window. She gazed out across the airport, watching planes arrive and depart. So many people, going to so many places... The sound of the engines was a constant thrumming in her ears, the chatter of other passengers passing across her head as she thought again over the events of the past few months.

It had been Aunt Chloe who had insisted on Tracy's taking a holiday. Tracy had been quite prepared to go on working for the autocratic author who had employed her ever since she left secretarial college. And he, of course, thinking only of his work amongst the dusty tomes of the library and museum, had been quite prepared to let her go on working. But Aunt Chloe, down from Yorkshire, had taken a firm line.

'Tracy needs a holiday,' she had told Mr Osborne, her face as implacable as her voice. 'She's had a very hard time these past months, with her father so ill. I don't think you've had any idea of what she's been going through.'

'I know things have not been too easy,' Mr Osborne had protested, but Aunt Chloe swept this aside with a contemptuous snort.

'Not too easy indeed! The poor child's been labouring under a tremendous strain! Not that *that's* anything new for her – losing her mother when she was only five, brought up by a father who was never strong! It's a wonder she's managed to grow up normal at all.'

'Tracy seems an eminently well-balanced young lady to me,' Mr Osborne ventured; like almost everyone else, he was completely intimidated by Tracy's formidable aunt.

'Well balanced – that remains to be seen! She seems to be far *too* well balanced, if you ask me!' Aunt Chloe declared. 'Too much responsibility too young, that's Tracy's trouble. It's made her serious. And Tracy's not the serious type. She ought to be full of life, bubbling over with it – instead, she's stuck here with you, poring over old books and spending half her life back in the past. And her home life hasn't helped, taking care of poor Bob all those years. Oh, I know they loved each other dearly and Bob never complained – but it's no life for a young girl. And now – well, as I say, the past few months have been more than any child of twenty should be expected to cope with.'

Tracy had resented the 'child' label – after all, as Aunt Chloe herself had just pointed out, she had been forced to grow up years before her time. But she also felt a stirring of something like excitement as her aunt spoke – excitement at the thought of Life bubbling inside her – like fizzy champagne, quiet in its bottle until the cork was removed and then bursting joyously forth, a sudden foam of happiness and laughter. And then, hard on the heels of that thought, came the memory of the past few months with her father – and the bubbles died within her, leaving her feeling as numb and empty as she had felt on the day he died.

It had been a long illness, and Tracy had known for a long time that it would eventually kill her father. The word 'leukaemia', avoided by many, became by deliberate intent a familiar one to them. Robert Pelham had never wanted his daughter to fear death and had never shown any fear of it himself – whether he actually felt any, nobody would ever know. Throughout the long years, he had remained cheerful and Tracy, hurrying home every evening from the elegant Georgian house where she worked with Mr Osborne, to the tiny cottage in the Herefordshire countryside where her father had elected to spend his last days, had never felt the need for anyone else in her life. She scarcely remembered her mother, although she kept her photograph by her bed and her father spoke of his dead wife frequently. But to Tracy she was little more than an idea; the gentle father who had looked after her so tenderly ever since she could remember, was all her life.

The knowledge that death would come had not in any way lessened her sadness when eventually she had realised that her father's increasing weakness would not, this time, be averted by a remission. Bob Pelham had waited with cheerful resignation; Tracy had endured an increasing agony of mind and spirit that she dared not reveal. She could make no plans, as her father had urged her to do, for her own future; she could not look ahead without pain and preferred to live entirely in the present, bringing her father as much happiness as she could reap for him during that last autumn.

He had died just after Christmas – a Christmas which Tracy would never forget, when each had tried to make the other happy. Tracy hoped that she had succeeded; she only knew that her father's efforts had brought her close to tears on more than one occasion and that even now she could not recall them without an ache in her throat.

She scarcely remembered the rest of the winter; it seemed to have passed almost unnoticed, a gloomy memory of driving through cold and fog to Mr Osborne's house, accompanying him to the dimmest rooms of the library for research, returning at night to a cottage that was now empty and strangely cold, in spite of the central heating that had been installed when they first moved in. Even the coming of spring had meant little to Tracy. And then Aunt Chloe had arrived, and insisted on a holiday.

'It's the only thing,' she had said, brushing aside all Tracy's protests. 'Mr Osborne will just have to manage without you. It will do

18

him good… Now, where will you go?'

'I don't *want–*' Tracy began, and then gave in. It was too much effort to combat Aunt Chloe when she had made up her mind, and she suddenly remembered her father once saying, ruefully, that nobody had ever got the better of his strong-minded sister. 'Well, I suppose I could go and stay with Peggy.'

'Is that one of your friends? The one in Devon? Not a bad idea, I suppose, but – no, Tracy, it won't do. I want you to get right away. Somewhere completely different, where you will be forced to think, to take notice. Not somewhere where you will be wrapped up in cotton-wool and sympathy. That would be the worst thing for you – you need a cold, fresh air to blow away all your cobwebs and give you a new start. It would be a good thing if you could move away from here entirely and get a new job, something a bit livelier than the one you've got, but I suppose you won't consider that…'

'No, I won't,' Tracy told her, as firmly as she could manage. The thought of selling up her home and leaving all that was left of her life with her father, appalled her. 'I'll go on holiday if you insist, but I won't leave the cottage – or Mr Osborne.'

'Hmm. Well, perhaps you'll change your

mind. Or someone may change it for you... Meanwhile, *I'll* arrange a holiday – I'm not having you taking fright and running off to Devon, that'll do you no good at all. Leave it to me.' And because she couldn't summon up any real interest in holidays, Tracy had left it to her.

Nevertheless, the news that Aunt Chloe had arranged a fortnight in Yugoslavia had come as a considerable shock and jerked her out of her apathy. Tracy had stared at her triumphant aunt and thought wildly of arguments against the idea.

'Yugoslavia! What on earth made you choose there? I don't know a thing about it – I've never *heard* of anyone going to Yugoslavia! It's not a holiday place!'

'Nonsense – of course it is. Thousands of people go there. It's a beautiful country, Tracy, you'll love it, and it's different enough to take you right out of yourself.'

'I don't know that I want to be taken out of myself. Honestly, Aunt Chloe, I don't know a thing about Yugoslavia. I don't even know the names of any of the towns.'

'Really, Tracy, you do talk rubbish,' her aunt said briskly. 'You've heard of Dubrovnik, surely? And Belgrade? And the Adriatic coast? It's tremendously popular.'

'Am I going there?' Tracy said doubtfully, acknowledging that she had heard of Dubrovnik and Belgrade.

'Well, not there actually. I've booked you at a hotel right up in the Julian Alps. The most beautiful scenery – look – and close to the Austrian and Italian borders. Now, do stop making difficulties and look as if you're going to enjoy yourself, Tracy. I don't *have* to come down here all the way from Yorkshire to do this, you know!'

And Tracy, immediately contrite, had begged forgiveness for her ingratitude and allowed her aunt to have a thoroughly good time in fitting her out for the holiday. Together, they applied for a passport, bought clothes and a new suitcase, packed. And then Aunt Chloe had seen her off on the London train at Hereford and driven back in Tracy's small car to the cottage, where she intended to spend the next fortnight in spring-cleaning, ready for her niece's return.

Tracy brought her mind back to the present. The engines had taken on a new, more urgent note, and her heart began to thump in sympathy. She turned to Nick and he smiled reassuringly.

'Be taking off soon. Here comes the

stewardess to see if you've fastened your seat belt – and you haven't, naughty girl! Look, let me do it–' His hands fumbled for a moment at her waist and Tracy sat very still, trying to keep the faint colour from her cheeks. Nick moved away slightly and smiled at her. 'All safe and sound now, not scared?'

She shook her head and his smile broadened. She was aware of admiration in his gaze, although quite unconscious of its cause. Tracy was one of those rare people who are pleased with their own passport photographs; the small heart-shaped face beneath the short fair curls, the direct gaze and the slightly enquiring set of eyes and mouth had seemed exactly what she saw in her mirror every day. She did not see, as Nick did, the impishness in her grey-green eyes, the glow of her fair complexion and the sparkle that even sadness had been unable entirely to dim; and she had no idea at all as to what these qualities could do to a male heart.

The engines throbbed faster, their note rising and the plane began to move forward, smoothly and slowly at first, then with increasing speed. Tracy braced herself; felt a warm hand clasp her own and, as the ground suddenly dropped away below them, clasped it in return. The plane climbed steadily until the ground was like a map spread out beneath them and it seemed that they must go for ever into the sky; then it levelled out, a few wisps of cloud floated between them and the green fields, and Tracy let out her breath in a long sigh.

'There,' Nick said, keeping her hand clasped firmly in his. 'That wasn't so bad, was it?'

'No – no, it wasn't.' Tracy relaxed, smiling a little self-consciously. 'It's beautiful.' Her nervousness vanished and she leaned eagerly against the window, staring down at the countryside spread below. 'Look – oh, look, isn't that Windsor Castle?'

'Yes. And there's the Thames, see? And – oh, we're climbing again. We'll probably go above the cloud – you won't see much then, I'm afraid.'

'I hope we don't have cloud all the way,' Tracy remarked as the plane swept up through a dense grey fog. And then they were above it, sailing through an intensely blue sky with the white foamy clouds beneath them. 'Although this is lovely too. I shall never be afraid of flying again.'

'A lot of people worry about take-off and

landing,' Nick told her. 'But it's over in a few minutes – the flying itself is a marvellous experience.'

Tracy nodded and turned back to the window. Gazing out of it made a good camouflage for her thoughts. She had to admit that it looked as if Aunt Chloe might have been right – already, the experience of travelling, flying and meeting new people (she resolutely pushed from her mind the memory of the handsome, arrogant Scot) had begun to dim a little the pain and sadness of recent months, to put her life back into some sort of perspective. Perhaps the strange surrounding of a foreign country would help complete the cure – and although Tracy did not realise it, the very fact that she was now able to admit the need for some kind of 'cure' indicated that she was already on the path to recovery.

Once everyone was settled and the plane flying smoothly, the dark-haired Yugoslavian steward and his pretty companion stewardess came along with drinks. Nick bought two cans of lager and showed Tracy how to use the small table on the back of the seat in front. They sipped their drinks, laughing and chatting companionably, and Tracy thought dreamily how fortunate she was to have met such a congenial travelling companion.

'Which hotel are you staying at?' Nick enquired as they began to eat the salad lunches brought round by the busy steward. By now, they were flying over Belgium and most of the cloud had disappeared, but Tracy found it difficult to eat, gaze from the window and talk to Nick all at the same time. She chose to eat and talk, and smiled at her companion.

'The Kranj, at Belanice. What are you laughing at?'

'Only your pronunciation,' he grinned. 'And I've no right to laugh at you at all. I happen to have a friend who has been to Slovenia several times and gave me a quick course in pronunciation! It's fairly easy – you don't sound the "j" at the end of a word, so Kranj is just "Kran". In the middle of a word, it sounds like a "y" – like in "L-yubl-yana". And the "ce" is a sort of "chay" – "Bella-nee-chay" – see?'

'I see – yes, it does sound better. More fluid, somehow. I didn't think "Bella-nice" sounded right, somehow.' Tracy joined in his laughter. 'What a good thing I met you!' And then she wished she hadn't said it, for Nick's eyes darkened with an intent look that brought a blush to her cheek. Hastily, she turned back to the window and exclaimed in sudden wonder.

'Look – oh, Nick, look! It must be the Alps!'

Nick peered over her shoulder. 'Yes, it must be. What a marvellous sight.'

Ahead and on the skyline rose the first tips of the Alps, white peaks tipped here and there with the black of bare rock. The purity of the untrodden snow reflected the blue of the sky, so that it appeared tinged with the icy colour, as they flew nearer and lower over the mountains it seemed to Tracy that the whole world was composed of range after range of stark beauty, the mountains stretching away into the far distance, with green fields and forests only a memory, or a dream. Here and there were ridges where perhaps one could walk, part of that spectacular landscape; yet there seemed no possible means of reaching them, and Tracy wondered whether those isolated wastes had ever known the tread of human foot or shaken to the cry of a human voice.

She shivered suddenly and drew back from the window, catching Nick's glance as she did so.

'They are beautiful,' she said slowly, 'But

so immense. I never dreamed... One could wander for a lifetime there and never see another person.'

'You couldn't survive there for long,' Nick said soberly. 'Not a good place for a crash-landing.' His eyes twinkled so that she wouldn't take his words too seriously, and he continued quickly, 'But we're not going to have to worry about that. I hope we're going to see a lot of one another in the next couple of weeks.' His hand found hers and clasped it again, warmly. 'I didn't tell you – I'm at the Kranj as well, so you needn't think you'll be able to escape!'

Tracy smiled at him. But behind the heart-shaped face a few doubts were beginning to form. Nick was fun, she liked him – but did she want to get involved? As yet, Tracy had never had a serious boy-friend – her work with Mr Osborne had given her little opportunity to meet young men, and she had been too concerned with her father either to want or need much social life. She had certainly not come on this holiday with thoughts of romance in her mind. And then she chided herself – after all, what had Nick said or done to make her think like this? He was simply alone on holiday, as she was herself, and pleased to find someone young and congenial to talk to. It certainly seemed, as she glanced around the plane, that most of their fellow-travellers were middle-aged or older.

But, as Tracy looked over her shoulder, her idle glance met a stare that was beginning to become as familiar as it was disconcerting. A pair of icy blue eyes met hers, faintly sardonic, definitely hostile; locked and held for what seemed an eternity. Tracy felt a cold shiver run right through her body. She took in the contempt of the other's gaze – and then tore her own away and stared determinedly out of the window, praying that her colour would subside and her heart stop thumping before Nick noticed that there was something amiss.

She had thought that the arrogant Scot had been left behind at the airport, never to cross her path again. Yet here he was, on the same flight to Ljubljana, heading perhaps for the same ultimate destination as she and Nick, and she wondered again whether she had been really wise to come on this unexpected holiday.

TWO

Nick's voice interrupted her thoughts. Her hand was still in his, and she felt the pressure of his fingers as he pointed out of the window.

'We've passed the Alps – we must be almost there. Look at the valleys, Tracy – they're like wide green roads running into the mountains.'

'And the lakes,' Tracy breathed, gazing down at the green valleys between the grey, rugged mountains. 'It really is beautiful. Aunt Chloe was quite right.'

'Who?' Nick sounded startled, and Tracy laughed, feeling suddenly light-hearted. After all, what did one rude Scotsman matter – they probably wouldn't see each other again.

'My Aunt Chloe. She persuaded me to come. Oh – we're going down!' Her words ended with a squeak as the plane descended sharply. Nick had already seen that her safety belt was fastened and she clung un-ashamedly to his hand as the aircraft

29

dropped. Her ears throbbed in unison with the engines and she closed her eyes, filled suddenly with panic – and then, with a soft thump, the plane had landed and Tracy opened her eyes to find that they were taxiing across a small aerodrome, ringed by grass and fir trees, under an incredibly blue sky.

'Good heavens,' she said, peering out. 'We're the only plane here!'

'Bit different to London, isn't it?' Nick grinned. 'Well, that's all over till next time. Super flight, wasn't it?'

'Lovely.' Tracy followed him along the gangway and down the steps into the sudden warmth of the afternoon. Beyond the dark green of the conifers and etched sharply against the blue sky she saw the jagged peaks of snow-covered mountains. Nearer at hand, the airport buildings lay low and quiet. There were few people about as the passengers entered, and Tracy received a strong impression that the staff had come in only to welcome the passengers from this particular plane. There was none of the frantic bustle, the pushing crowds, the near-chaotic hullabaloo of London. Following Nick, she handed over her passport to be stamped by an efficient Yugoslavian girl, then walked through to the entrance hall, where their luggage was circling round on a conveyor belt.

'There's mine!' Tracy hurried past Nick to where a large green suitcase was appearing, and grabbed it before it could pass. She pulled it from the belt and set it down on the floor.

'Thank you, that's *my* suitcase,' a deep voice said close beside her; and Tracy, half-recognising the burr, whirled to find the arrogant Scot beside her. His eyes were steely as before, his face like a handsome mask of stone. He held out his hand.

'My suitcase, if you don't mind.'

'I'm sorry, you're making a mistake,' Tracy said coldly. 'This happens to be *my* suit-case!' Really, the man was insufferable.

'Indeed it is not.' He bent and twisted the label. Tracy looked down and felt her face flame. 'You see, Iain Ross Macalister, Edinburgh. Bound for the Kranj Hotel, Belanice.' He straightened up. 'Perhaps now you'll believe me – unless you think I crept into the luggage hold during the flight for some strange purpose of my own, and put my label on to *your* suitcase!'

'It was an easy enough mistake to make,' Tracy protested hotly, her embarrassed

31

apologies dying on her lips at his sarcasm. 'I'm not trying to steal your suitcase, for heaven's sake! It just happens to look like mine.'

'I had assumed that,' he told her. 'Probably this is yours about to pass us now.' And with an ease that shook Tracy – who knew just how heavy her suitcase was – he reached out a long arm and flicked her own green case from the belt. He bent again and glanced at the label; and when he straightened, there was a sardonic twist to his mouth.

'I take it that you are *Miss* Tracy Pelham, of Hereford?' His glance flicked past her to Nick, who had collected his own luggage and was now standing close by, a puzzled look on his face. 'Then this is indeed yours. And now I see that your – *escort* – has arrived, so you'll have no further need of my services.' He glanced down again at the suitcase with its green label. 'It seems that whether we like it or not, we are about to be thrown together, since we are both staying at the same hotel, – however, it will no doubt be large enough to enable us to avoid further embarrassment!' And with a final curt nod, he wheeled and strode away to the doors, through which Tracy could see him already boarding the coach that waited to take them on the next stage of their journey.

'Well,' she gasped. 'Of all the pompous, conceited – all I'd done was take his suitcase by mistake, and he treated me as if I was trying to *steal* it! I've never met such a rude arrogant man!'

'He certainly seems to have got across you,' Nick said. 'I wouldn't have thought you capable of such strong feelings! Don't tell me you've got a temper!'

'No, I haven't – at least, I never thought I had! But I could cheerfully strangle that man – he seems intent on being unpleasant to me!'

'Oh well,' Nick said with a shrug. 'I shouldn't bother about him – after all, he's nothing to you. Let's get these cases out to the coach. It looks as if we're the last.'

And that was another black mark against them, at least as far as the Scot was concerned, Tracy thought as she climbed aboard and met his inimical stare. She tried to return the gaze levelly, but as their eyes locked a shiver ran through her and she turned hastily aside. Iain Ross Macalister, whoever he was, had an altogether strange effect on her – one that she disliked and distrusted – and the best thing she could do was to keep well out of his way. Not even to look at him. And having made up her mind to that effect, she tossed her head and turned to stare deliberately out of the opposite window.

Because she and Nick had boarded the coach last, the only two seats left were separated. Tracy found herself next to an elderly lady, who smiled politely and made pleasant small-talk as they bowled along the quiet roads. Tracy would have preferred to look out at the scenery they were passing, admiring the range of mountains far away on their right and the wide green fields and forests they passed. Here and there, a group of women were working in the fields, dressed in voluminous black. An ox, great head bent, drew a plough across the rich earth. Villages with steep-roofed houses and churches with tall narrow towers and onion-shaped domes passed across her view. But she could exclaim over none of these, for her companion had by now embarked on a long description of her son's children, whom Tracy gathered were the apple of their grandmother's eye, but outrageously spoiled by their mother. She was relieved when the coach turned into a small town and stopped outside a large hotel, and her companion began to gather up her possessions.

'We are now in Bled,' the courier announced; she was a pretty Dutch girl who had welcomed the passengers aboard just before Nick and Tracy had arrived but had had little to say since. 'Here I shall be leaving those who continue to Belanice. You will be taken for the rest of your journey in a minibus, and I hope you have very happy holidays!'

Tracy realised that everyone was getting off the coach. She stood up hastily, smiled at the lady with the grandchildren – she could not for the life of her recall whether the woman had told her her name – and glanced round for Nick. Then she scolded herself – it was absurd to rely on a total stranger in this way, however attractive and friendly he might be. There was no reason at all to suppose that he wanted to be encumbered with her all the time, having befriended her in the plane. She turned to search for her luggage and make sure it was put into the minibus, and found Iain Macalister beside her.

'Alone?' he remarked coolly, and Tracy felt her face grow warm.

'Is it any business of yours?' she asked coldly.

'I just thought it seemed a little odd that your so-attentive escort should have deserted you.' His glance flicked over her, taking in every detail of her slim figure in the pale green trouser suit. 'After all, you have scarcely arrived – Miss Pelham.' He looked past her and Tracy turned to see Nick chatting with some animation to the Dutch courier. She turned back to Iain Macalister puzzled; then met the sardonic gaze, caught the slightly raised eyebrow and realised with a flash of insight exactly what he was thinking.

The blood rushed to her face and she opened her mouth to tell him, indignantly; that Nick was *not* her boy-friend, that they were not on holiday together – and then she paused. After all, what business was it of his? And why should she care what he thought? Let him think what he liked – it didn't matter a scrap to her!

'If, as you implied earlier, Mr Macalister, you wish to have as little as possible to do with me,' she said icily, 'then I wonder why you take so many opportunities for conversation.' She noted with satisfaction the dark colour rise in his cheeks, then smiled sweetly and added, 'As you said, there is no real need why we should even have to acknowledge each other's existence. Until this morning, we had never even met.' And she turned away, walked over to the minibus and climbed into the front seat.

It was the first time Tracy had ever spoken to anyone in that way, and the effort left her feeling exhausted. She sat staring ahead, her heart thudding almost into her throat, her eyes smarting. Impatiently, she brushed at them with the back of her hand, and became aware of the other passengers climbing aboard the minibus.

She had expected that Nick would take the seat beside her, but owing to a misunderstanding with the driver, found that he was sitting just behind. She turned to smile at him – and saw that Iain Macalister was taking the one remaining seat, in the front. She would be sitting close to him all the way to Belanice, pressed between him and the driver! Silently she groaned. What on earth had possessed her to get into the front?

The driver of the minibus was a young Yugoslav with black curls and a cheerful expression. He chatted easily in good English as he swung the vehicle through the narrow streets of the quaint town, showing the passengers the old buildings, the beautiful lake with its red-topped church on a tree covered island, the castle high on the cliffs the other side. Bled was a popular holiday resort for Yugoslavs as well as foreigners, he told them, and pointed out President Tito's summer residence, sheltered behind high walls. Tracy gazed about her, fascinated, and tried to forget the antagonism between her and the tall, dark Scot who sat so close, his thigh almost touching hers.

The road was now running beside a river, its green waters foaming over dark rocks as it rushed along the narrow bed. On the other side of the road was a railway, and above them rose steep cliffs, covered with dark green conifers. Tracy stared up at them, awed. Coming from the borders of Wales, she was accustomed to hilly and often wild scenery, but she had never seen anything like this spectacular, almost relentless land.

'Here there is room only for the river, the road and the railway,' the driver told her. 'But you will see many places where the road twists just as much although there is no narrow valley. We say it is because too much road was bought to go between Bled and Belanice, and so it must be twisted to make it fit in.'

Tracy laughed and relaxed, then was immediately and unpleasantly aware of Iain Macalister. A tremor ran through her body; she glanced up at him, caught his unsmiling glance and turned hurriedly away. She looked back at Nick for reassurance and his brown eyes smiled into hers.

Iain Macalister was speaking now, and with a small shock Tracy realised that he was speaking in one of the Yugoslavian languages. The driver answered him rapidly and she listened, fascinated, wondering how any Englishman could ever learn such a difficult-sounding language. Or any Scot, she corrected herself wryly. She decided that he must have been here before, many times, and then deliberately put the thought of him out of her head and gazed at the scenery.

The journey took about an hour, taking them further into the mountains. There was still snow on the peaks, enhancing their rugged beauty; below the snowline grey rocks ran down to the dark green of conifer, skirted on the lower slopes by the fresh colour of newly leafed hazel and beech. The road ran into and out of villages, and at last the minibus slowed, approaching a wide lake. The driver slowed down to give them all a better view, and Tracy exclaimed with pleasure at the sight of the great calm sheet of water with its ring of encircling mountains reflected in the blue depths. Nearby, the river ran out of the lake under an old stone bridge, and just across the bridge stood a cream-painted church with a tall, narrow tower topped with a red minaret.

'It's lovely,' Tracy said softly. 'If we had to go home now, I'd still be glad I came!' She was aware of Iain Macalister's sudden glance, but she was too enraptured to care. No Scot, however arrogant and pompous, was going to spoil this moment!

Half an hour later, Tracy stood on the balcony of her room, gazing out over the lake. The hotel stood on a rocky, wooded knoll above the village. It was built like a large chalet, with stone walls and a wooden roof, and each room possessed its own wooden balcony with flowered window box.

Aunt Chloe had certainly done well. Tracy was ready to admit now that a holiday was just what she needed – and this one looked like being exactly right for her. She was glad now that her Aunt had not booked a fortnight on the Adriatic coast, remarking in her forthright manner that she 'didn't want young Tracy idling the time away on a beach, she could do that at Torquay!' Here, there would be no idling; already the mountains were producing in Tracy a restless longing to get out and walk, to explore the valleys and the tracks. She had always loved walking and so had her father, although in recent years his frailty had prevented them from taking the long walks they would both have enjoyed. Each knowing that it could never be, they had talked of walking in the Black Mountains and Brecon Beacons; and a lump rose in Tracy's throat as she thought of how he would have revelled in this beautiful scenery, with the mountains rising almost sheer out of the lake, their snowy peaks reflected in the water far below.

'Hey! Don't you want any dinner?' Tracy jumped and looked down. Nick was standing on the path below, laughing at her, and with a smile and a quick wave she ran back through the bedroom, down the stairs and joined him. He smiled at her.

'I thought you'd be goggling at the view,' he said. 'Marvellous, isn't it?'

'Beautiful. Have you done any climbing, Nick?'

He glanced at her and seemed to hesitate.

'Oh, a bit here and there,' he said casually. 'Not an awful lot. Why – you don't want to have a go, do you?'

'Oh, no – I'm not all that keen on heights. I'd probably panic! I just thought – it looks such good country for climbing, I wondered if that was why you'd come.'

'No, not this time. I'm just here on an ordinary holiday, same as you. Actually, I was supposed to be coming with a friend – but he cried off at the last minute. So I had to come alone, and you can't climb alone. Not safe. Look, the table by the window's vacant, shall we grab it before someone else does?'

Tracy took her seat, gazing with interest around the room. Like her bedroom, it was sufficiently 'different' to be quite definitely foreign. The walls were wood panelled, and the windows double glazed, with several inches between the two panes. The broad sills were filled with plants, and on the tables were small jars containing lily-of-the-valley.

'Oh, my favourite flower,' Tracy exclaimed, sniffing at them with pleasure. She glanced up and saw Nick smiling at her; and as she smiled back, his gaze grew disturbingly intent, leaving her with a slightly

42

breathless feeling.

'Tracy,' he said, and paused. 'Tracy. You – you don't mind my assuming we'll eat together, do you?'

'Of course not,' she answered. 'I'm glad you want to. It's rather miserable, eating alone in a room full of people.' And she suddenly wondered who would be eating with Iain Macalister – or whether he would be sitting alone, fixing her every now and then with that strange brooding gaze.

'And shall we do a bit of sight-seeing together?' Nick continued eagerly. 'Walking – whatever you want to do? Do say yes, Tracy.'

'Yes – all right. If you want to.' She smiled at him again and he suddenly leaned forward, looking at her closely.

'Do you know, when you smile like that your nose wrinkles? It's rather sweet.' He picked two or three lilies out of the jar and smelt them. 'And these are just right for you – natural, unspoilt and lovely. You're lovely, Tracy – has anyone ever told you that?' He tucked the flowers behind her ear. 'Don't look so scared. I'm not going to eat you! Here comes our dinner – and it looks far more appetising!'

Light was already filtering through the gauzy

curtains next morning when Tracy woke, and she rolled over to look at her watch. Half-past five! She burrowed back into her pillow, determined to have a good long sleep this morning after the long journey of the day before, but sleep refused to return.

It was probably because it was a strange place, she decided, getting out of bed and padding across to the window. Drawn back, the curtains revealed once more the spectacular panorama of the mountains, tipped with the rosy colour of the rising sun. Faint shreds of early mist swathed about them like diaphanous scarves, and the lake shimmered like pewter in the pale light.

Tracy gazed at it for some moments and then slipped back to bed, but she was now wide awake. She looked again at her watch – six o'clock. Well, breakfast started at seven – a hideously early time, she'd thought, seeing it on the hotel card last night, but since she was awake so early she might as well make use of it and have an early start.

She was glad now that she had made no firm plans with Nick for this morning. His behaviour at dinner last night had disturbed her; again, she had the strong feeling that, nice though he might be, she wasn't yet ready to become involved with any man.

Too much had happened to her recently to have any trust in her own judgements. She refused to believe that Nick himself could at this stage have any strong feelings beyond a certain attraction for her, but she was afraid that her own heart might betray her.

After dinner they had explored the hotel and found a notice stating that their courier would be in the hotel after breakfast, at nine this morning. There were no tours or expeditions included in the price of the holiday, but trips were arranged for each day which they could go on if they wished. The courier would be able to tell them about these and also give information on the various walks and places of interest in the immediate vicinity. Tracy and Nick, in common with most of the other guests, had agreed to be there to meet the courier, and Tracy looked forward to finding out as much as she could about the whole area.

Slowly, savouring the fact that for once there was no hurry, she showered and dressed, choosing pale blue slacks and a gingham shirt. She brushed her short, curly hair, slipped her feet into sandals and ran lightly down the stairs to the dining room.

To her surprise, although it was only just seven, several people were already there and had begun their breakfast of rolls and coffee. Tracy sat down, smiling a good morning to those she recognised, and began to butter a roll. A shadow fell across her plate and she looked up, her heart thumping suddenly as she recognised Iain Macalister.

'I hope you slept well,' he remarked stiffly, and Tracy inclined her head.

'Very well, thank you, though I was surprised to wake so early.'

'You'll find you do, here. Everything starts earlier in Yugoslavia – the shops are all open by seven and the day is under way. It's because of the sun.'

'I see,' Tracy said politely, not having the least idea what he meant. He stood almost uncertainly beside her and she glanced up again. 'Was there anything else, Mr Macalister? Because you did say you wanted nothing to do with me. I really don't see–'

'I'm sorry,' he said abruptly, the ice returning to his eyes which had, for a few moments, looked warm and human. 'I merely made a polite inquiry. I'm sorry if it offended you.' And he wheeled away and made for his own table, where he sat with his back turned to her which for some reason disturbed her more than if he had been facing her.

After breakfast, Tracy went back to her room and finished unpacking, then she carried a chair out on to her balcony and sat gazing at the view. She felt she wanted to drink it all in, absorb it completely because when she returned to England, it would be all that there was left of this holiday. She must take a photograph – she must take several. Aunt Chloe had insisted on her bringing four rolls of film and now Tracy was grateful.

As she sat there, a low white sports car wound its way along the lakeside road. Tracy watched it with interest, which quickened as she saw it turn and climb the twisting road which led up the knoll to the hotel. For a few minutes, it disappeared among the trees; then it came into sight again, climbing the last stretch, and she saw that it was driven by a girl; a startlingly beautiful girl, even at that distance, with a mane of auburn hair.

The car stopped just below Tracy and she leaned out, watching the girl get out of the car. Her figure was set off to perfection by the turquoise sweater and pants that she wore, and Tracy could see that her eyes were large and dark – perhaps violet – and thickly-lashed. She leaned against the car, took out a briefcase and started to thumb through the contents.

Tracy realised that this was probably the courier and watched with increasing interest. And then she heard footsteps below and the girl turned quickly, with a smile of eager welcome lighting her already lovely face into breathtaking beauty.

'Darling!' she exclaimed and Tracy realised with surprise that she was English. 'How lovely to see you – it's been such a long time.' She held out her arms and a man stepped forward into Tracy's view. He took the girl in his arms and kissed her; and with a strange jerk of her heart, which she did not even want to attempt to analyse, Tracy realised that he was Iain Macalister.

THREE

Slowly, Tracy made her way to the terrace where they were to meet the courier. The discovery that the newcomer was English and on obviously intimate terms with Iain Macalister had had a strange effect on her, and she resented it. After all, why should she care about the Scot's friendship? Why should the sight of him kissing and being kissed by a beautiful redhead, and with obvious enthusiasm, so disturb her? *I'm just a frustrated spinster*, she told herself ruefully, *getting my thrills second-hand. Well, there's one good way of dealing with that!*

Accordingly, the first person she looked for on arriving at the terrace, was Nick. He was lounging against the balcony, gazing at the mountains, and Tracy paused for a moment to watch him. She noted his pleasant, brown face, the way his hair curled crisply at the nape of his neck, and she recalled his words about Romance. She was not at all sure that she was falling in love with him – but he was friendly and kind, and most important of all, trustworthy. Which was more, she suspected, than might be said of the arrogant Iain Macalister!

Nick turned suddenly and saw her watching him. His face lit up and he stretched out a hand.

'Come and sit beside me. I was just thinking how marvellous it must be to get right up into the mountains.'

'They're beautiful,' Tracy said, 'But wild

and dangerous too. Somehow implacable – as if anyone who trifled with them would be harshly dealt with.'

'Oh, they're all right so long as you're sensible,' Nick said easily. 'There are well-marked paths up most of them. Look – I went down to the village just now and got a map.' He unfolded it and spread it out on the table. Tracy gazed at it, picking out the hotel and the lake, her finger following the paths that wound across the hills, marked in red.

'You see, you can walk right up this one, to the ski hotel at the top.' Nick craned his head. 'You can see it up there, look, with the sun glinting on the windows. Then you can walk down by another path, to the village at the head of the lake and back along the shore.'

'There's still snow at the top,' Tracy remarked doubtfully.

'Oh, there won't be much now. I expect you can get through all right. And there's another good walk to the waterfall at the head of the lake. It's where the river comes down from the mountains. Quite a beauty spot. We must go there.'

'I'd like to have a look at the village too. It's fascinating to see the houses and how people live.'

'Let's do that this afternoon, then,' Nick suggested. 'By the time the courier's finished with us, it'll be almost lunchtime. We could have early lunch and then a nice long potter round the village afterwards.'

He seemed to have taken it for granted that they were to spend their time together. Tracy was aware that she was fortunate – the prospect of a lonely fortnight had been somewhat daunting. She smiled at him and was about to tell him this, when the rest of the party came chattering out on to the terrace.

Iain Macalister and the auburn-haired girl came last and Tracy heard Nick whistle softly. 'So this is our courier,' he murmured. 'And I see that our noble Scot has already taken charge of her. Look at the way he's holding her arm!'

Tracy had no wish to look, but she found her eyes drawn to the couple as they sat down at one of the small round tables. They certainly made a striking pair, Iain's dark hair and ice-blue eyes contrasting almost startlingly with the girl's Titian mane and violet eyes. Tracy was forced to admit that they both looked most attractive.

The girl smiled round at everyone and opened her briefcase.

'Good morning, and I hope you are enjoying your first sight of Slovenia – as you know, this is the most westerly republic of Yugoslavia. You will already have discovered how beautiful it is and I want to help you to discover more, either for yourselves or by joining some of the many excursions arranged for the coming weeks. My name, by the way, is Melissa, and as you can tell I am English–' the guests laughed politely '–and this is my second year as courier in Belanice so if there is anything you need to know, please don't hesitate to ask.'

'Isn't she a honey,' Nick murmured in Tracy's ear. 'I know one thing – if I'd not had any questions to ask before, I'd soon have thought of some – if I hadn't met you first!' And his hand squeezed hers.

Melissa was showing them a copy of the map, and Tracy twisted her head to see the paths as she pointed to them. It seemed that there were walks of all lengths, taking them to Alpine meadows, steep gorges, waterfalls and villages. But, Melissa warned them, there was still snow on some of the mountain tops. 'Don't try to take these paths,' she said, 'They are not at all safe. It is better to use the cable car.'

She then went on to tell them about the

various excursions by coach that would be leaving from the hotel during the next fortnight, and Tracy's imagination was caught by the idea of going to Lipice. This, Melissa told them, was the original stud where the famous Lippizaner horses of the Spanish Riding School of Vienna were bred.

'You can see the mares and foals, and the stallions will give a demonstration of their skills. It's a very interesting day, and we continue on to the coast afterwards, to give you a glimpse of the Adriatic seaboard.'

'I'd like to go on that trip,' Tracy said. 'I used to do a lot of riding at home.'

'I'd like to go to the Postojna caves,' Nick remarked. 'I'm not really a horsey type – but if you'd like to go, I'll go too!'

Tracy was not at all sure that she wanted a reluctant companion, but Melissa was now talking about the Three Countries Tour, taking in Austria and Italy, and she listened with interest – although she had already realised that the high cost of the trips would prevent her from making more than one or two, and that she would have to satisfy herself on the whole with exploring the country nearer at hand.

She watched the beautiful courier, admitting reluctantly that the English girl did have a very appealing manner. Iain Macalister certainly seemed to find it so; he was sitting close beside her, his face softer than Tracy would have believed possible. She found herself searching his eyes for the cold glint that had been in them as he had watched her yesterday, and wondering how it would be to be looked at as he was looking at Melissa now. And then, as if aware of her gaze, he turned his head and for a moment the softness remained in his eyes as his glance met hers. For a split second they stared at each other and a strange emotion twisted in Tracy's heart; then the moment had passed, the ice returned to the cold blue eyes and the dark-haired Scot turned his head away, just slowly enough to sear Tracy with the humiliating impression that she didn't even warrant a hasty movement.

Melissa had now finished her talk and was taking bookings for the various trips.

'What about it?' Nick was asking. 'Lipice? The Caves? Three Countries? You name it.'

'I'd like to go to Lipice. I'll leave the others – perhaps I'll go to the caves next week. Otherwise, I'm quite happy to wander about here. Anyway, Nick, I'll make my own bookings – yes, I can't let you do it. And you mustn't think you have to spend all your time with me, you know. I don't mind being alone.'

The brown eyes looked hurt. 'Of course I want to be with you. Unless you don't want me?' And he gazed at her with such a look of doggy devotion that she laughed, and hadn't the heart to tell him that she might, at times, prefer to roam entirely on her own.

The rest of the morning was spent in wandering down to the lake and hanging over the bridge, watching the fish dart in the water amongst the weeds. The sun was warm on Tracy's back and for the first time for many months she began to feel again the zest for life which her father's illness and death had taken from her. Her eyes, reflecting the green of the lake and rushing river, took on a new sparkle as she smiled and laughed at Nick, and she was quite un-aware of the turmoil that they were capable of causing.

The village of Belanice proved every bit as enchanting as Tracy had hoped. They began by exploring the church – open today because it was Sunday although usually, Melissa had told them, it was kept locked – and Tracy gasped in wonder at the richness of the decorations. Outside the church had been plain, its cream-washed walls shabby and peeling; inside it was a welter of gilded statues, richly framed pictures and gold candelabra. Even the domed ceiling was covered in paintings, and there was not an inch of bare wall to be seen anywhere.

'I would never have dreamed it was like this,' Tracy whispered. 'It's overwhelming!'

'Takes your mind off the sermon, though,' Nick remarked, staring round at the dozens of statues. 'No wonder this was a poor country – all the money went into furnishing the churches!'

'I prefer our plain churches, though,' Tracy said soberly as they came out into the bright sunshine. 'There's something much more *solid* about them, somehow. More down to earth.'

They wandered on along the narrow street, passing newly-built houses – many of them large and elegant. Tracy and Nick stopped to admire each one, comparing them with houses in England. They decided that these must be the equivalent of expensive executive-style houses at home, built to order, and not the property of ordinary villagers.

'This is all new development,' Nick said as they strolled along. 'The real old village is further in – tucked away round the shoulder of the hill.'

'Yes – older cottages. But there are still some new ones being built. Look, they've already moved into the ground floor although the second floor hasn't been finished yet! I suppose it's quite a sensible idea.' Tracey stopped and looked up at the bare bricks. 'I like the houses, Nick. They're attractive.'

'And always room for the cow, you notice!' Nick indicated the lean-to shed at the side of each house and, peering into one, Tracy saw that there was indeed a cow there, lying on clean straw, its body brown and glossy. 'They keep them in all winter and take them up on the pastures in summer. I suppose they don't consider it's warm enough yet!'

The village was larger than they realised, its many narrow streets and alleyways twisting between the houses. Tracy exclaimed in delight over the many quaint corners, and used over half of her first film. She was especially pleased with a tiny, chattering stream that wound its way through the street, crossed by small wooden bridges between the gardens, and stopped to photograph it.

It was as she lowered the camera that her eye was caught by a flash of brilliant colour some distance away – the brilliant electric colour of a kingfisher on an English river; turquoise and coppery red.

She turned her head slowly and saw, between two steep-roofed cottages, the slender figure of Melissa, still clad in her close-fitting sweater and pants. She had evidently not seen Tracy and Nick, but was laughing up into the face of the man beside her. He was in shadow, but Tracy had no doubt as to who he was; and as she watched, he stepped out into the full light of the sun.

It was, just as she had known it would be, Iain Macalister; and as Tracy stood transfixed, staring after them, the couple joined hands and knocked on the door of the house nearest to them.

'Well, what d'you make of that?' Tracy was aware of Nick beside her, staring with interest as Iain and Melissa disappeared through the dark doorway. 'Friends of the pretty courier? And I must say the strong silent Scot seems to have got well in with her very quickly.'

Tracy wondered whether she should tell Nick that Iain and Melissa had obviously known each other before, then dismissed the idea. There was nothing to be gained by discussing the man – he was, as she had told herself yesterday, a mere irritation and not worth the time spent in discussion. Impatient with herself for even bothering to watch him, she turned away and walked quickly up the narrow street towards the end of the village.

'Hey, what's the hurry?' Nick caught her up and took her hand, swinging it in his own. 'Want to walk up the hill to the valley that Melissa told us about?'

'If you like,' Tracy said shortly. 'I don't mind.' And then, ashamed, 'Yes, please, Nick, that will be lovely.'

He glanced down at her and Tracy blushed, aware that he was amused. She bit her lip and stared ahead, walking rapidly. They were out of the village now and climbing the gradual, grassy slope towards the green beechwoods.

'I'm sorry,' Tracy said after a moment. 'I'm a bit edgy still.' She wondered if she should tell him about her father, but knew that it would be dishonest to give him the impression that grief was the cause of her bad temper – although she was far from clear in her own mind as to the real cause. It was just that Iain Macalister got under her skin, somehow. Whenever she saw him, she felt at a disadvantage; and even though he had been unaware of her presence a few minutes ago, she knew that if he had seen her he would have considered her to be spying. And Tracy had an uncomfortable feeling that he would have been justified.

The path led them above the village, where they could look down on the huddle of rooftops. It was very peaceful. Beyond the village, the minaret of the little church was etched against the lake, and past that lay the mountains, grey and rugged, their snowy summits gleaming in the sunshine. Around them, they could hear the constant chirping of grasshoppers, loud as birds; and in the woods cuckoos called.

'Have you ever heard so many cuckoos!' Nick exclaimed, and Tracy laughed and admitted that she had not. 'They woke me at five this morning. Dozens of them! Well, at least three. I swear they go around in flocks!'

They walked on through the woods, the ground carpeted with spring flowers. The sun poked long fingers of gold through the trees, dappling the air with light. Somewhere below, they could hear the sound of rushing water.

'It's the gorge,' Tracy said, peering down. 'Oh, we must see it!'

'Look for a path leading to the left.' Nick

was ahead, pushing through the soft tangle where new-leafed branches reached across the path. 'Here we are. I can see a bridge down there ... now – look, Tracy.'

'Oh!' For a moment, she was speechless. The beauty of the scene overwhelmed her. She was accustomed to the sight of mountain streams and rock waterfalls in Wales, but this was on a scale so different that it took her breath away.

From somewhere high in the hillside, the stream came tumbling through the trees, carving itself a deep gorge in the black, glistening rock. Now a pale ice-green, now the sparkling white of a glacier, it foamed and crashed under the sheer cliffs, covering the great slabs of rock that lay below with a shifting, gleaming shine of water. Here and there, persistent sunbeams found a target, lighting the dark rock with gold and the water with a flash of diamond; and constantly, as it had done for thousands of years without a pause for the little activities of mankind, the timeless roar of the water filled the narrow gorge with sound, echoing in Tracy's ears like the symphony of a great composer.

There was nothing to be said. Silently, she took Nick's hand and silently they walked back along the banks of the gorge, pausing again and again to gaze at the rushing, foaming waters beneath them. Other people passed them and smiled, but Tracy could find no words of greeting. She was thankful that Nick seemed to sense and understand her need for silence; small talk or meaning-less chatter would have shattered the spell of the moment. Perhaps, she thought, her father would have been the only person capable of communicating with her just then – but even of that, she could not be sure. Perhaps there was nobody; perhaps this was a time when one could only be alone.

The path drew gradually away from the gorge, and Tracy found herself beside Nick on the road back into the village. The tumult of sound died away. She blinked and smiled at him, feeling that she had just emerged from a dream, and they walked companionably back through the narrow streets.

'This really is quite a place,' Nick re-marked, 'I feel as if I've just climbed a mountain – inspired but exhausted! How about a drink?'

'I'd love one,' Tracy admitted. 'But where?'

'One thing I've already realised about

Yugoslavia is that every village has a café!' Nick waved an airy hand. 'And here it is. Open too!' He led Tracy through the door and they sat down at a small table. 'Now, what's it to be? Got your phrase book?'

'I've learned the word for coffee,' Tracy smiled. *'Kava. Bela kava* – white coffee.'

'Aren't you going to try the local speciality – *slivovica?* Plum brandy? You can't leave Yugoslavia without trying it at least once, although I suspect it's an acquired taste and needs practise!'

'Well, I'll practise another day. Today, I'd like coffee.'

They were served by a pleasant-faced Yugoslavian girl with dark hair and friendly eyes. She shook her head smilingly at Nick's attempts to order coffee, agreeing that coffee was available, but not *bela.*

'Turske,' she insisted; and since she spoke no English, Nick finally nodded his head.

'All right, *turske,* whatever that is.' A thought struck him. 'Oh course, there are no licensing laws here. I could have a beer.'

'Oh, I know what that's called,' Tracy exclaimed, *'Pivo.* Ask her for that.'

'Pivo?' Nick said to the girl, and she nodded enthusiastically, broke into a torrent of words none of which was understood by

either Nick or Tracy, and disappeared into the kitchen.

'Well, all we have to do now is wait and see what we've ordered!' Nick remarked. 'I wonder what *turske* is. Anyway, if you don't like it you can always have a sip of my *pivo!*'

Tracy gazed with interest at the cup the waitress was now carrying out of the kitchen. Topped with a huge puff of whipped cream, it certainly smelt like coffee. But when she gently edged the cream away with her spoon, the liquid beneath looked more like thick cocoa.

'Oh, it's Turkish coffee!' she discovered. 'Of course – *turske*. It's probably as strong as ship's cocoa!' She sipped it cautiously; strong coffee was not her favourite drink. 'Mm – it's rather nice, so long as you get the cream too. I shouldn't like it on its own. What's your *pivo* like?'

'Beer,' he said, grinning, and they sat slowly sipping their drinks and enjoying the sounds of the strange language that emanated from the kitchen.

Tracy turned slightly to gaze out of the window. The village street was empty; a few chickens scraped in the dust on the other side of the road, and a broad-shouldered man, clad in jeans and a check shirt, was stacking logs in an open shed beside one of the houses. With a slight shock, Tracy realised that the next house was the one that she had seen Iain Macalister go into, with Melissa; and even as the thought came into her mind, she saw the door open and an old woman emerge, her face leathery and wrinkled but split with a wide smile as she talked to the two who followed.

Melissa came out first and stood on the rough road, as flamboyant and out of place as a kingfisher in a farmyard. She turned as Iain followed her, smiling up into his face, and once again Tracy wondered what it must be like to have a man like Iain Macalister, his normal expression as forbidding as that of a particularly grim stone statue, look at one like that. She could hardly blame him for reserving his smiles for Melissa, however; the courier was not only elegant and beautiful, her smile was also warm and delightfully sincere. Tracy gazed enviously at the mane of auburn hair, a shade that she had always especially admired, and unconsciously ran her hand through her own short curls. Most of the time, she preferred to have short hair, which was just as well since grown long her own became a wild tangle; but occasionally, and particularly when confronted with someone like Melissa, she yearned for long hair which could be brushed till it shone and combed into elaborate coiffures.

Iain and Melissa were saying goodbye to the Yugoslavian woman. They had obviously spent the entire afternoon in the cottage, and Tracy wondered why. Absorbed with curiosity, she watched as they turned away – and then flushed scarlet as Iain looked directly at the café and saw her.

His expression changed at once. For a long moment, during which Tracy found it impossible to take her eyes from his, he stared at her. His thick, dark brows drew together in a look of intense displeasure; his lips clamped tight and Tracy could see the twitch of a small muscle in his cheek. Then, as coldly and indifferently as if she had been a total and very uninteresting stranger, he turned slowly away, took Melissa's hand and tucked it into his arm. They walked away together down the narrow street and Tracy, conscious of a strange burning sensation behind her eyes, watched them go.

She became aware of Nick's voice, reading the price list on the wall, and realised thankfully that he had not noticed the other two at all, being absorbed in an effort to decipher the strange names. Tracy turned from the window and got out her own phrase book, but could only find one or two words in it.

'I know why it is,' she decided at last, resolutely pushing the picture of Iain Macalister's expression from her mind. 'The phrase book is in Serbo-Croat, which is the main language of the country – and the notices and price lists are in Slovenian, which is the language here! The only thing that seems to be common everywhere is President Tito's portrait!'

'Yes, I'd noticed that. There was one in the shop this morning – one at the hotel – and one here. They certainly think a lot of him, don't they?'

'And he was Slovenian.' Tracy remembered snippets from the books she had read about the country before coming on holiday. 'I suppose it was probably in these mountains that he hid during the war, when the Resistance was doing so much. It must have been very different here then.'

Nick glanced at her cup and offered her another coffee, which she laughingly declined. 'One *turske* is enough for me,' she smiled, and they got up to go.

The walk back to the hotel was pleasant,

and again they strolled beside the river –
much wider now that it had escaped from
the narrow rocky gorge. It ran beside the
road, veering away as they approached the
bridge, and they stood for a while watching
where it foamed into the stream running
from the lake. Tracy threw a stick in and
mused as it swirled away across the rocks.

'All the way to the Danube,' she said. 'Do
you think my stick will get there? And along
the Danube itself – through Vienna – it
seems very strange that a river can start in
one country and end in another.'

Nick reached out and ruffled her hair.
'You're sweet,' he said affectionately, and a
sudden unreasonable irritation rose in
Tracy. She didn't want to be told she was
sweet; she wanted something else, just as by
the gorge she had needed someone with
whom she could really communicate.
Abruptly, she turned away and walked
quickly across the bridge; and then, feeling
ashamed, she stopped and smiled at Nick as
he fell into step beside her. After all, she had
no right to expect anything from him, other
than companionship.

Nick grinned back cheerfully, evidently
quite unaware of the brief moment of dis-
cord. He took Tracy's hand and swung it

easily as they stopped to gaze up the length of the lake. On either side the mountains rose, grey and implacable, their lower slopes covered thickly with trees. There was beauty there; the wild, relentless beauty of untamed landscape, awesome and immense. Tracy felt her spirit rising to meet it's challenge, and she drew a deep breath.

'How about a walk along the lake and up to the waterfall tomorrow?' Nick suggested. 'We can get a packed lunch from the hotel and spend the whole day out. Fancy it?'

His words seemed banal in connection with the spectacular surroundings, but Tracy longed to explore and she smiled eagerly at him.

'That would be marvellous. It all looks so beautiful. We'll need months to explore properly!'

Nick looked at her strangely. 'Well,' he said with an enigmatic smile. 'I suppose there'll be other years.'

Tracy felt a faint blush on her cheeks. She glanced hastily at her watch and exclaimed at the time; and Nick, still with a smile on his lips, allowed her to lead him away from the lake and back to the hotel.

Tracy was thankful to regain the privacy of

her own room. She closed the door behind her, leaned against it and surveyed her small domain, enjoying the feeling of space and coolness imparted by the gauzy curtains and the low furniture. A comfortable armchair awaited her; but Tracy kicked off her shoes and lay down on the bed, determined to sort out her impressions of the afternoon.

Deliberately, she went over again every step of their walk beside the gorge, recalling the way the water had flowed through the narrow chasm, green where the sun lit it and almost black as it dived through rocks hollowed by centuries of force. Once more, the roar of water against rock filled her head; the chirruping of grasshoppers against the silence of the hills, the constant repetitive call of the cuckoos – all these she recalled, but try as she would, she could hold none of these memories for more than a few moments. Through it all came the picture of a dark, unsmiling face, ice-blue eyes staring into hers, a mask of granite turned suddenly human as it rested on the lovely oval face of a girl dressed like a kingfisher, with a mane of auburn hair...

Impatiently, Tracy sat up and swung her legs off the bed. She would have a shower, dress herself up for the evening. Iain

Macalister was never to know the turmoil he caused within her whenever she saw or thought of him. He was never to know the breathlessness that caught at her throat when he turned that stony gaze upon her; the flutter of her heart and the strange twists that it performed when she saw him smiling at the beautiful Melissa, taking her hand and tucking it into his arm with that curiously intimate gesture. No – Iain Macalister had been nothing but a thorn in her side since the moment he had cannoned into her at the airport lounge, spilling coffee on his immaculate grey suit. And Tracy had an uncomfortable feeling that he knew it and was enjoying the situation; that whenever he suspected she had forgotten his presence, he took pains to remind her, to humiliate her afresh.

But he would do it no more, she decided, stepping under the shower. From now on, Iain Macalister was to mean no more to her than a – a fly on the wall. Whatever his relationship with Melissa – whatever his reasons for spending the afternoon in the cottage of an elderly Yugoslavian woman – none of it was to mean a thing to Tracy Pelham, fresh from the Herefordshire countryside, who had other fish to fry...

FOUR

The journey to Lipice was a long one and meant an early start. Tracy was amused to think that at home the thought of boarding a coach at six-fifteen in the morning would have appalled her. Yet here, it had already become quite normal to be up and about by five-thirty or six, taking a short walk and still arriving for breakfast by seven.

Perhaps in a town hotel, with a lively night life, things might have been different. But here in quiet Belanice, everyone seemed to go to bed soon after ten; Tracy had been glad to say goodnight to Nick and slip into her own room at an hour which at home would have seemed childishly early. She wondered if she would be able to keep up the routine when she returned home; it was pleasant to be up so early, she reflected as she dressed, and pleasant to be already out soon after eight, with the whole day in front of one.

Yesterday's walk, planned as an excursion to the famous waterfall, had become after all a lazy stroll by the lake where, finding a sheltered bay, she and Nick had stopped to swim and sunbathe. It had been a pleasant day, happy and carefree. Tracy had, true to her resolve, managed to keep thoughts of Iain Macalister out of her mind, and she had seen neither him nor Melissa at dinner. Free from his antagonistic presence, she had relaxed and been able to enjoy Nick's simple, uncomplicated friendship. They had swum, lain in the sun on soft, springy grass, fed ducks remarkably similar in their appearance and behaviour to English ones, and let the hours slip by in a warm haze of holiday idleness. It had been the first such day Tracy could remember for a long time, and the memory of it was still warm within her.

She dried herself after her shower, blessing Aunt Chloe for arranging that she should have her own adjoining bathroom, and considered what she should wear. It would probably be hot later; they would also be spending some hours in the coach and a time at the stud, as well as a visit to the coast. Eventually, she chose a pair of light grey slacks and a sleeveless yellow shirt, with a pale grey pullover in case it turned chilly in the evening. As an afterthought, she

73

pushed her bikini and a towel into the bag –
she hated arriving at the seaside without
swimming gear.

Packed breakfasts had been given them
the evening before, and Tracy decided that
she had time to eat hers now. She spread a
roll with butter and filled it with ham, sitting
on her balcony to enjoy the view as she ate.
The sun was just tipping the mountains
with early morning pink, and the lake lay as
still as a mirror below.

The early morning silence was broken
suddenly by the sound of cheerful voices, as
people began to come out of the hotel and
stand about in groups, waiting for the
coach. Tracy hastily finished her roll and
took her chair back inside. She had noticed
that Iain Macalister was one of those
waiting and she did not intend to incur his
displeasure again by being late for the coach
a second time!

However, when she ran lightly out of the
hotel and joined the group, the coach had
still not arrived and Iain seemed scarcely
aware of her presence. He gave her a curt
nod, his eyes rapidly passing over her so that
she was unsure as to whether he now knew
every detail of her appearance or had hardly
noticed her at all! Then he turned back to

the elderly man he was talking to, and continued his conversation.

The coach wound into view on the road below the hotel and the murmur of conversation rose as people discussed the trip.

'Of course, I've been to Vienna itself and seen the actual Spanish Riding School,' a woman whom Tracy knew as Mrs Andrews remarked, rather loftily. 'Quite beautiful. And the horses have been to Earls Court too, you know.'

'I've never seen them,' Tracy said.

'Oh, well, you'll love it then. Especially if you're fond of horses. Ah, here's your young man.' And Mrs Andrews turned away to talk to her own companion, a tweedy woman called Miss Johnson, who looked like a schoolmistress.

Blushing slightly, Tracy turned to greet Nick as he came hurrying up to her. She had not realised that they had been so firmly coupled together by other guests at the hotel, but supposed it was inevitable. After all, they had spent all their time together since meeting at the airport. She turned slightly and found Iain Macalister's gaze on her, as hostile as ever, his sardonic mouth curled with faint contempt... Flushing, and with a toss of her head, Tracy turned away and smiled at Nick.

'I thought you were going to be left behind,' she said, still aware of Iain's gaze like a gimlet boring into her back. 'Have you had your breakfast?'

'Good lord no – I've only just got up!' He grinned at her. 'Next time we make a date for this hour, I'll get you to come and wake me. I must have been more sleepy than I thought after yesterday.'

The party climbed into the coach, talking and laughing, and they set off. Nick un-packed his rolls at once and began to eat, while Tracy gazed out of the window. The coach filled with the subdued hum of conversation, rather like the sound of bees on a hot summer's day. Before her eyes the fields, woods and mountains passed like a panoramic film. Tracy's head nodded; dimly she realised she was falling asleep, but she had no energy to wake herself up. She was half-aware of her head slipping on to Nick's shoulder, and then she knew no more.

She slept for over an hour, unaware of the amused glances of other passengers, the scenery they passed through or even the fact that Nick's arm was round her shoulders holding her firmly against him. She woke at last with a jerk, to find herself staring be-musedly out of the window at grey buildings and bustling streets.

'Where are we?' She stared about her, confused; for a moment she thought herself in some strange English town, and then she saw a road sign written in an unfamiliar language, and her memory returned. She found Nick's arm about her and turned to look at him. He was laughing at her, his brown eyes merry, and she couldn't help smiling back.

'I wondered where we were. Have I been asleep?'

'For over an hour,' he told her. 'We're in Ljubljana. Not very spectacular, is it?'

Tracy stared out of the window. Ljubljana, she decided, was like any other small capital city. Probably there were more attractive, interesting parts; but if there were, the coach driver did not seem disposed to drive through them. They passed large areas of bare, untended ground where blocks of flats stood isolated, though a few were sur-rounded by pleasant lawns and play areas for the children. There were plenty of shops – mostly supermarkets, just as you might find in any suburban area – and the occasional school. Tracy was conscious of a feeling of disappointment.

'It could be anywhere,' she said crossly, still only half awake. 'Foreign towns ought to *look* foreign!'

The journey continued, leaving Ljubljana behind. Now they were running along a broad, modern road, past wide fields with no hedges. Women were working in small patches, hoeing and sometimes ploughing or digging new areas of earth. Everywhere stood the wooden drying racks used to store hay when it was cut – empty now, like large rustic climbing frames. Occasionally a village could be seen, red roofs clustered together with the tall church tower as their focal point, and once or twice a romantic fairy-tale castle appeared on the skyline, remote and mysterious.

'We'll be at Lipice soon,' Nick remarked, and as if to prove his words the coach swung off the main road along a narrow lane signposted 'Lipice'. Tracy woke properly at this and sat up eagerly, gazing out in the hope of seeing the horses. They were obviously approaching the stud; wooden fences lined the road and the fields were cropped close. But they saw no horses until they entered the grounds.

'There they are!' Tracy turned quickly and

followed the pointing finger. A cry of delight rose to her lips and she watched the horses – grey and white mares accompanied by small, dark-bodied foals. They were cantering across the fields, manes and tails flying, wheeling to gallop in the opposite direction, running together with an easy stride that told of high breeding.

The coach drew into a large car park and stopped. Melissa, who had been sitting in the front with Iain and the driver stood up. 'I expect you'll all be glad of a drink now,' she said in her friendly way. 'The hotel café is open and they have a very good souvenir shop too. You may leave your lunches in the coach and come to collect them after the performance. We'll meet outside the café in half an hour to look round the stud.'

Tracy stood by the coach, gazing around. The area was shaded by beautiful old oak and lime trees. Along one side stood the long frontage of the hotel, with tables on the terrace and bright umbrellas. And a little way off she could see the buildings of the stud itself – the place where the famous Lippizaner horses were bred. Even as she looked, two of them passed her, drawing a smartly-painted trap.

'I can see you're a horsey type,' Nick

observed, the mocking glint in his eyes. 'Can you spare time for a coffee, do you think? *Turske?* Or would you prefer a cold drink?'

Tracy realised suddenly that it was very hot. 'Oh, cold please. I'm sorry, Nick. I do rather love horses. I used to ride a lot before–' She stopped suddenly, the treacherous pain mounting inside her, and turned away. She still couldn't talk about her father to Nick, though she knew that he would have been sympathetic.

'Sit there,' he said, guiding her to a table. 'I won't be long.'

Tracy sat down, shading her eyes from the sun and gazing across towards the paddocks. Herefordshire seemed a long way away. She closed her eyes, resting them from the glare of the sun, and became aware that a shadow had fallen across her. Nick, with the drinks, she thought lazily, and without opening her eyes said, 'Nick, you *are* nice to me. I don't know what I'd do without you!'

'Well, I'm afraid you're going to have to manage for a while yet,' a voice told her dryly, and at the familiar – and despised – Scot's drawl, Tracy's eyes flew open. 'Can you not make do with me for a bit?'

'Mr Macalister!' Tracy gasped. 'I thought – I thought you–'

'You thought I was the young Lochinvar,' he finished mockingly. 'Well, I'm afraid it's just the old satyr. Will it be so terrible to bear with my company for a few minutes until your – protector – gets back?'

'He is not my *protector*, whatever that may mean,' Tracy said stiffly. 'We merely enjoy each other's company.'

'Is that all?' He raised one eyebrow, looking distinctly amused, and Tracy felt a shiver of dislike run through her body. Why couldn't the man leave her alone?

'Is there nowhere else for you to sit?' she enquired coldly. 'Shouldn't you be with your – companion?' She left a pause before saying the last word, and had the satisfaction of seeing his face darken with annoyance.

'Touché,' he said after a moment. 'Look, Miss Pelham – why don't we call it a truce? Put a stop to all this sword-crossing? We're here to enjoy ourselves, after all.'

'I'm sure that you *are* enjoying yourself, Mr Macalister,' she rejoined. 'And whether or not we are on speaking terms cannot make any possible difference to you. After all, we mean nothing at all to one another.' Her heart beat fast as she spoke, making her slightly breathless, but she lifted her chin and looked him straight in the eye as she finished, and had the satisfaction – though it gave her a queer pang as well – of seeing his eyes cloud, as if she had hurt him somehow. Which was ridiculous, she told herself sharply; the man was incapable of being hurt.

'Very well,' he said, his voice flat. 'If that's how you want it–'

'I really can't see why you bother with me at all,' Tracy said, smiling sweetly. 'And here comes my *protector* with our drinks. Good morning, Mr Macalister.'

The Scot stood up and for a moment, Tracy sat gazing up at the two men, so different from each other. Iain Macalister was a good six inches taller than Nick – he must be over six feet, she thought confusedly – and beside his muscular frame, with his thick black hair and brows, his stern arrogant face, Nick looked scarcely more than a boy. The brown eyes were just as merry, the grin as infectious – but it looked lightweight now, as if he were only playing at life, whereas Iain Macalister seemed somehow to have been tried and tried sorely. The discovery came as a shock to Tracy. For a moment she wished desperately that she had not been so unequivocally rude; and she was just about to make some sort of apology when Iain said curtly, 'I must go now. I doubt if our paths will cross again. I wish you a happy holiday, Miss Pelham.' He turned on his heel, nodded to Nick and walked quickly away.

'What's the matter with him?' Nick asked, setting down the drinks. 'He always seems to be hanging round you – or looking at you. Isn't he satisfied with the beautiful Melissa?'

'Oh, he doesn't think of me in that light!' Tracy answered, forcing a laugh. 'In fact, I don't really know why he bothers to speak to me at all – he hates the sight of me!'

'Nonsense – nobody could do that.' Nick smiled at her across his glass. 'Anyway, you don't worry about his opinions, do you? Forget him, Tracy – the man's obviously got neither taste nor manners. Drink up now, we'll have to be off soon to do our tour round this stud you're dying to see.'

The party gathered outside the café and moved off towards the paddocks. Tracy saw that the buildings were surrounded by an old wall, its plaster peeling and flaking in the hot sun. Inside the enclosure were large buildings – probably stables – and to one side was a large modern building which looked rather like a sports stadium.

'That's the Riding School,' said a voice beside her and Tracy turned, surprised to find Melissa regarding her with friendly eyes. 'You're fond of horses?' the courier continued.

'Yes – I love them.' Tracy was nonplussed, feeling obscurely that the tension between her and Iain must surely have been communicated to the girl who so obviously held his affections. But Melissa seemed as natural and friendly as if she and Tracy had known each other for years. She began to explain how the stud had been started in 1580 by the Austrian Archduke Charles.

'He was the son of Emperor Ferdinand. You know, of course, that Slovenia was for a long time under Austrian rule. That is why there is such a strong connection with Vienna.' By now the crowd had thickened round them and everyone was listening to Melissa's little lecture. 'The foals are jet black when they are born, and as they grow the colour lightens – first to brown, then gradually to grey and eventually in the best of them to a pure white. The finest stallions are sent to Vienna, or remain here for performances and for breeding. The less good – which are still magnificent horses – are gelded and sold as riding or carriage horses.

And the mares, of course, remain here to produce foals, keeping the breed alive.'

Tracy smiled and thanked Melissa, for now the official guide had taken over and, since he was speaking mostly in German, she would have had little chance of understanding him. Tracy had already come to the conclusion that German was a far more useful language than her schoolgirl French – almost all the Yugoslavs knew German and Nick, who confessed his knowledge of it to be quite slight, was able to make himself understood far better than she was.

Slowly, the group – now a large one, having been joined by several other coach parties – made its way around the stud. It was difficult to remain with one person and Tracy found herself separated from Nick; however, she needed no one to share with her a delight in the lovely mild-eyed mares with their milk-white coats, and the dark foals who seldom strayed from their mother's sides but reached out enquiring necks to sniff at the visitor's hands.

The stallions were kept separately, standing in cool stables. They were tall and heavily-built, their rear quarters showing the power that was needed in their performance, for Tracy could remember seeing pictures of them holding rearing positions that would have severely damaged the backs of most horses. Their eyes were not mild and nobody ventured close to them, but admired their beauty from a discreet distance.

By the time she reached a large, empty courtyard, Tracy had lost sight of Nick altogether. She did not worry about this, being too much taken up with photographing two mares that had just been led in; and then her heart leapt with delight as, with a cry of warning, a groom appeared from a pair of huge doors at the far end of the courtyard and pulled them open.

The courtyard was suddenly full of horses, white mares and black foals. They spread like a wave across the yard, thundering past Tracy in a stampede of whinnying movement. Then they were all at the end, foals huddled close to their mothers, staring with huge velvet eyes as the visitors gathered round to photograph them.

Tracy felt a sharp tug at her elbow and turned, expecting to see Nick. But it was the groom; a small, friendly man with a wizened face. He grinned at her and whispered confidentially, 'You come this way – I show you in school first!' And still clinging to her arm, he scuttled off across the yard.

Tracy followed, bewildered but interested, and found herself led through a large stable, where stallions turned inquisitive eyes as they passed. She had scarcely become accustomed to the darkness when she was in the sunlight again, blinking; and then, before she knew where she was, in the cool, spacious foyer of the large building she had seen before.

'Riding School,' the guide explained proudly. 'You find a good seat now. That way!' As he pointed up some steps and gave Tracy a sharp push.

Amused but uncertain, Tracy made her way up the steps and found herself looking down at a vast, sand-covered arena. The opposite wall was full of windows, so that the whole place was light and airy; on the side where Tracy was were rows of seats, arranged in tiers just as they would be in the sports stadium she had at first taken it for.

For a moment, she was the only person there. Then she heard the others approaching, their laughter and chatter filling the air, and then that sound was lost in a sudden burst of music – a Strauss waltz, coming from loudspeakers somewhere – and Tracy decided that she had better find a seat. She ran lightly down the steps to the front row and settled herself about halfway along.

The rest of the visitors began to throng inside. Tracy craned her neck, looking for Nick afraid that he might have been hurt by her apparent desertion. But although more and more people arrived and the hall was soon almost full, she could see no sign of him. She had been keeping her bag beside her on the bench to reserve the seat; now, realising that he must have come in unnoticed and already found a seat elsewhere, she removed it.

'May I sit here?' a deep voice enquired, and Tracy, without looking round, answered, 'Yes, of course. I was keeping it for a friend but he must have already sat somewhere else. I – oh!'

Iain Macalister looked into her eyes, faintly smiling. 'I take it that it was not I for whom you were keeping the seat!'

'You know it wasn't!' she retorted furiously. 'Oh, why don't you leave me alone? You say you want nothing to do with me, and then you keep – *pestering* me! Is it some sort of game you're playing – this taunting? Are you the sort of man who torments kittens and ties cans to dogs' tails?'

His smile vanished. 'Indeed, I am not. And

I have no intention of taunting you, either. Or pestering you, as you call it. I merely don't see any need for this constant bickering.'

'Well, *I* didn't start it!' Tracy began, and then stopped, recalling that, this time at any rate, she probably *had* started it. She turned away, conscious of the scarlet colour in her cheeks, aware that he was amused and all the more infuriated by the knowledge.

Why did he have this strange effect on her – this need to assert herself, to leave him in no doubt that as far as she was concerned, his existence was of no importance at all? Tracy could not remember ever having felt like this before. She knew that she was behaving badly – but somehow, whenever she saw or spoke to this man, met the icy blue of his eyes or listened to his Scottish drawl, a strange emotion threatened to overwhelm her – an emotion she was quite unfamiliar with and unprepared for, and which made her want to fight, to see him turn away in the knowledge that over her, at least, he had no mastery.

It was his arrogance that caused it, she thought. His air of authority, of always being right; his self-confidence and sheer, unshakable conceit.

She began to rise, with the intention of finding somewhere else to sit, but his hand gripped her wrist like a clamp of steel.

'Don't be so childish! You'll never find a seat now, and it won't hurt you to sit with me for a few minutes. I'm not contaminated, you know – and it might help you to grow up, to sit next to a *real* man for a while, and not an immature boy!'

Furiously, Tracy tried to twist her hand away, but his fingers tightened and she stifled a cry of pain. 'You won't make a scene here,' he muttered, his voice hard and angry. 'The performance is just about to start– Now, *sit still* – and enjoy yourself!'

Enjoy herself! Shaking all over with fury and that other, nameless emotion which threatened to force her to helpless tears, Tracy sat pinned close to his side by that merciless hand. The hall was now full and the music playing more softly. The audience was hushed and expectant. In a moment, she knew, the great doors at the end would swing open and the beautiful white stallions of Lipice prance into view.

And she, who had looked forward to this moment so much, must endure it in the company of the only man she had ever met who hated her – the only man who had ever stirred this powerful, terrible emotion within her. Conscious of him with every fibre of her being – aware that his body touched hers, that his hand was gripping her wrist, that his breath was soft upon her cheek as he watched her– Tracy sat rigid, and longed for the performance, not yet even started, to end.

FIVE

The music faded and the air was hushed and still. Tracy sat, her hand still held firmly in the strong warm clasp of Iain Macalister, her heart beating rapidly. But there was nothing she could do about it. She turned her head, like everyone else, and watched the great doors at the end of the hall.

Slowly, they swung open and a ripple of delight ran through the crowd as the horses appeared. They entered in a long line, each bearing a rider in grey uniform. With long, even strides, they walked through to the centre of the hall and lined up facing the audience, and every rider removed his cap and bowed.

It was simple, yet moving, this sight of a dozen handsome grey stallions standing perfectly still, their heads bowed as were the heads of their riders, their bodies sleek and powerful, their legs supple and their immaculate hoofs shining against the smoothly-swept sand. Tracy gazed entranced, almost forgetting the hand that clasped hers; and then, as the horses began to move again, wheeling apart to form two large circles, she remembered her camera.

'Let me go!' she hissed in Iain's ear, and he turned slightly to glance down at her.

'Don't you like holding my hand?'

'You know I don't! And I'm not holding it – you're holding mine! Let *go*, please.'

'But I don't think I will,' he murmured infuriatingly. 'It's a nice little hand–' He lifted it, still clasped in his own and regarded it. 'So small and white – it makes mine look so very large, don't you think? I'll keep it for the time being.'

A wave of frustration and fury swept through Tracy. She pulled and twisted at her hand, but failed to free it from the hateful grasp. She could feel the colour rising in her cheeks as she glared into the blue eyes – no longer icy cold, she noticed, but now full of amusement.

'For two pins I'd slap your face,' she muttered, aware that soon people would begin to notice their quarrel. 'Please, will you let go? I want to take some photographs.'

He released her immediately, and said contritely, 'Why on earth didn't you say so before? I just didn't want you to run away!'

Tracy threw him a withering glance before delving into her bag for the camera. The horses were now cantering in a circle, weaving a figure of eight, trotting, passing sideways between each other in a pattern so complicated that they must collide. Yet they never did. The whole performance took place in silence; there was no word, no crack of a whip, no apparent movement from the riders, who sat their mounts as tranquilly as if they were truly a part of the horse. Tracy watched with delight, completely absorbed now. She took picture after picture and almost forgot the man who sat at her side.

The gates swung open again and the line passed out. Tracy sighed and laid the camera on her lap. For a few moments, she felt that she had been transported from her own everyday existence into a world of fairy-tale, where white horses reigned supreme and music and dancing were the order of the day. Against this, everyday cares and worries seemed petty; quarrels and differences were an obscenity.

Now two stallions appeared, the two which Tracy had already picked out as the finest of all. Together, their heads held proudly, their riders calm as ever, they went through their own performance, moving together across the arena as closely as if in harness, perfectly in step and achieving a difficult passage – during which it seemed that they must surely trip over their own legs! – which had everyone applauding.

Tracy dropped her camera on her knee and clapped enthusiastically. She was aware that Iain was clapping too, and she turned to him, her face alight with the joy of the moment. For a moment they stared again into each other's eyes; but the hostility now was gone and Tracy was suddenly, disturbingly aware of him; and aware too of her own heart, which was jumping against her ribs in a very strange way.

'Beautiful, aren't they?' Iain said softly, still gazing into her eyes as if there were some truth that he must discover. 'I've never seen anything so beautiful.' And when he reached out once again and took Tracy's hand in his, his warm brown fingers clasped around hers, moving slightly in a gentle caress, Tracy made no effort to draw it back; and as the high gates swung open yet again, to admit the rest of the horses in their grand finale, she forgot her camera and sat quite still, caught up in a total magic such as she had never before experienced.

The music of Strauss filled the air, and the horses moved round in their now familiar pattern of circling, weaving, wheeling. But now they moved quickly, more lightly. Their sturdy bodies took on a new grace. Where a ballerina would spin and leap, the stallions, with a kind of dignified gaiety, turned and twisted, all four hooves in the air as the music commanded, with a neat little kick of the hind feet. Perfectly in time they created a ballet, a poetry of their own; and when at last the music ceased and they formed once again their long, grave line, Tracy was only half surprised to find her eyes wet with tears which threatened to spill on to her cheeks.

People were getting up to go. The performance was over. Tracy sat for a moment, strangely reluctant to move, afraid that the spell would break. And then, returning with a jerk to the present, she felt for her bag to find a handkerchief and realised that her hand was still closely held in that of Iain Macalister.

Embarrassed, she tried to pull it away, but he held it all the closer, drawing her round to face him.

'That,' he said seriously, 'is what is meant by poetry in motion.'

Tracy blinked. She had no wish to be caught once again in that strange, powerful interlocking gaze when his eyes seemed to probe to the very depths of her being. She tugged at his hand, trying to free her own; and abruptly, he let it go.

'Your escort is waiting for you by the steps,' he remarked, his voice suddenly hard. And, with a little, mocking bow, 'My thanks for the pleasure of your company. It was most – congenial.'

'I–' Tracy began, but stopped, with no idea as to what she had intended to say. His glance passed over her, as cold and indifferent as ever. The moment of accord had passed as if it had never been. And, feeling her eyes smart with a new humiliation, Tracy turned abruptly and made for the steps.

She should never have let him touch her like that, hold her hand, humiliate her in that way! She felt cheap, degraded. For a while, sharing the beauty of the powerful white horses, she had known a peace, a feeling of 'rightness' that had not been hers since childhood, when her father had been well and strong and the shadow that threatened to overwhelm them had not yet appeared. It was strange – almost unthinkable – that this Scot should be able to impart this strong sense of security. But his behaviour subsequently had cast her down into a cold pit of sorrow far deeper than the one she had just begun to struggle out of.

Why *couldn't* he leave her alone? Desperately, Tracy looked round for Nick, suddenly convinced that only with him would she find the peace she sought. Only in his company – straightforward, predictable, merry – could she have any chance of finding happiness again.

Nick was standing by the steps which led from the riding hall, scrutinising the faces of all who passed him. As Tracy stared at him, taking in every detail of his ordinary, pleasant face, his twinkling brown eyes under the thatch of curls, his habitually cheerful expression, a wave of warmth engulfed her. Why on earth was she standing here, worrying about a rude, boorish Scotsman who apparently disliked her as much as she disliked him, and took a fiendish delight in taunting her? After this holiday, she would never see him again; but Nick, who had already shown clearly that he admired her, who was good company and who would never, she was sure, vent an unaccountable temper on a complete stranger – Nick was a very different kettle of fish.

Giving her treacherous eyes a final wipe with her hanky, Tracy summoned up her warmest smile and hurried through the crowd to meet him.

'There you are!' Nick exclaimed. His brown eyes lit up as he studied her still-flushed face. 'Where were you? I spent most of the performance trying to spot you!'

'Did you?' Tracy was faintly surprised that anyone could have thought of anything other than the horses. She recalled that she herself had been quite – well, almost – oblivious of the warm hand that had held hers. She had certainly not spent the time searching the crowd for a sight of Nick. Guiltily, and suddenly thankful that Nick had apparently not seen her, she said, 'I was right down at the front... Did you have a good view? Wasn't it marvellous?'

'Yes, I could see all right.' Nick put his hand under her arm and led her down the steps into the warm air. 'Of course, when you've seen this kind of thing once, you've seen it all! I quite like horses, but I couldn't sit and watch it night after night on the box like some people do.'

'Oh, but these are *special*.' Vainly, Tracy sought the words which would express her feeling as she had watched the stallions, proud and stately in their dance. And then, glancing sideways at Nick, she knew suddenly that no amount of words would convey to him the emotion which she had felt, and that this was one subject in which they would never find accord. To Nick, the performance had been mildly interesting – no more. To her – and, she realised with a shock, to Iain Macalister – it had been an experience, a touch of magic, lifting them together out of the ordinary world into a realm whose existence they had only previously dreamed of.

It was disconcerting to realise that she could have been so much in sympathy with the hateful Scot, whereas with Nick the experience was almost a barrier between them. But only if I let it, she told herself fiercely. After all, it doesn't *matter* that Nick doesn't feel as I did about the horses. It doesn't *matter* that Iain did. None of us will ever be here again – all together. It doesn't mean a thing as far as real life is concerned.

But it was sad, nonetheless.

'What d'you want to do now?' Nick enquired as they walked slowly along the sun-baked path. 'Go back to the café? Have lunch? Look round the souvenir shop?'

'Well,' Tracy hesitated. 'What I'd really like to do is go and talk to some of those mares and foals in the paddock. But don't come if you don't want to. I'll meet you later, by the coach.'

'Nonsense,' he said cheerfully. 'Of course I'm coming with you. You don't think I'm losing you again, do you?' They wandered on to the paddock, where a number of snowy mares grazed, their sooty foals incongruous beside them. 'It's hard to believe they'll grow up white isn't it?' he added, staring at the graceful little animals.

Tracy bent and pulled up some grass to feed a yearling which had already approached the fence, its velvety muzzle poked enquiringly over the top.

'It's just the same as the stuff you've got there,' she told it as it grasped eagerly at the bundle. 'Oh, look, they're all coming now. Whyever didn't I bring some sugar?'

Nick lounged against the fence, watching

her good-naturedly as she petted the grey and black heads, and Tracy felt a rush of affection for him. So he didn't find any magic in watching them perform – but how much did that really matter? Wasn't it more important that he should be able to join in activities which might not hold any special appeal for him, yet still impart his own brand of cheerfulness to them? Many men, she knew – and amongst them, she suspected, the arrogant Scot – would simply refuse to come on any trip which did not interest them; yet Nick, who must have known that he would probably be bored for a large part of the day, had come willingly, just to be in her company. And if he were bored now, he was certainly not showing it. His brown eyes rested appreciatively on her slim figure in the grey slacks and yellow shirt and as Tracy turned to him, smilingly, her arms about the heads of a mare and a coal-black foal, his expression changed.

'Can I use your camera, Tracy? I must take a picture of you with those two.'

'Of course.' Delighted, Tracy held the position as he took the camera from her bag.

'Now,' he said, putting it away again, having taken three different photos, 'we shall have to keep in touch after the holiday. I shall want a copy of each one!' He moved over to Tracy and looked down at her, his brown eyes more serious than she had ever seen them. 'We *will* keep in touch, won't we? You won't disappear again into deepest Herefordshire, so that I can't find you.'

'I won't disappear,' she told him, slightly breathless. 'I'd like to keep in touch with you, Nick.'

Slowly, companionably, they walked back through the enclosure to the hotel. The sun beat down, hotter than ever, and they found a table at the end of the terrace, shaded by huge old oaks. Tracy sat down, gazing around her, while Nick went to the coach to fetch their lunch.

Some of the other passengers from their coach were sitting near and smiled at her. Tracy was beginning to recognise them now, and feel pleasantly familiar with them. She noticed Mrs Andrews, eating her lunch and laughing with an elderly couple from Nottingham. A foursome from Devonshire were feeding small pieces of ham to a stray cat which rubbed round their legs and miaowed in the way of cats everywhere. A large party of Dutch people – there were a great many Dutch, she noticed vaguely –

were roaring with laughter at some incomprehensible joke as they sprawled on the grass under the trees. And then, glancing idly past them, Tracy noticed Iain Macalister, sitting alone at a table on the very end of the terrace. He was staring down into his drink. As she watched, he looked up, watching the Dutch party. And with a queer twist of her heart, Tracy realised that his expression was no longer arrogant, no longer proud and self-contained – but as lost and lonely as that of a small boy left out at a party; defenceless, young and terribly vulnerable.

'Here we are!' Nick's voice brought her back to earth. 'Lunch – good old rubber ham and cheese! Don't these Yugoslavians ever have anything else on picnics? And I've got some drinks too. You'll need about a gallon to wash this lot down!'

Tracy laughed, unpacking the plastic carrier bags that seemed to be standard packaging for picnic foods – even the children took them to school with them and everyone on the terrace had their own. 'I thought it was a marvellous lunch the first day,' she said, taking out a large thick slice of bread and slapping an equally thick slice of ham on it, 'But I must admit it does begin to pall a bit!'

'Never mind, anything goes when you're hungry and at least it's wholesome.' Nick bit into his open sandwich. 'Bound for the coast next, aren't we? Better not eat too much of this solid fare if we're going to swim!'

They sat on the terrace until it was time to go; and only then did Tracy allow her eyes to stray once more to that end table where Iain Macalister had sat alone. But he had gone; and Tracy, feeling curiously deflated, wondered if he was now back with Melissa; and whether he still wore that strange brooding expression that had so oddly disturbed her heart.

It was growing dark when they finally returned to Belanice. Tracy, sun-warmed and pleasantly tired, sat beside Nick in the coach. Her hand was resting in his, her head leaning lightly against his shoulder. She felt relaxed, at ease and once again, mentally, she thanked Aunt Chloe for insisting that she come away for this holiday. Already, the cares of the past months were fading into a kind of proportion; and although she knew that she would never be able to forget her love for her father, or the pain of her loss, she knew also that life, which had seemed such a burden to her only a short while ago, could again be filled with joy and happiness.

She turned her head slightly to look up at Nick; and as she did so, his lips, so close already to her cheek, came down on hers in a gentle kiss.

'Oh!' Tracy murmured, shaken; in her thoughts, she had not yet reached as far as this.

'Oh, Tracy,' he murmured, his lips against her hair. 'Tracy, don't say no … Tracy, you're so lovely…' And he was kissing her again, more urgently now, so that Tracy drew back, frantically aware of the other passengers.

'Not now,' she whispered in a panic, although reason told her that nobody was likely to be watching them in the dim coach. She pushed at his chest and he released his hold on her, drawing away a little. Afraid that she had offended him, Tracy glanced up; but his expression was smiling.

'All right,' he whispered back, drawing her closer against him once more. 'Not now. But later – you and I, Tracy, have got some talking to do.'

Tracy stared out of the window at the darkening landscape. She was aware now that Nick believed himself, at least, to be in love with her. In fact, she admitted ruefully, she ought to have realised it before. That afternoon, for instance, as they had strolled along the main street of Portoroz – so much like Torquay that you could almost have believed yourself back in Devonshire! – and Nick had insisted on stopping to gaze into the windows of jewellers' shops. Tracy had been very taken with some of the bracelets and necklaces in pretty, filigree silver; but Nick had seemed to be more interested in rings...

And then there had been the moment when, lying on the beach just after a bathe in the warm blue sea, Tracy had caught Nick's eyes on her way in a way that spoke of more than admiration. Blushingly aware that he was about to speak, she had jumped up and run back into the water – and Nick had followed, laughing but determined and caught her to him as she floated on the rippling waves, so that they almost sank together...

Yes, she should have realised that a day like this could not pass without a kiss. And she chided herself now for taking it too seriously. After all, what girl of twenty in these days had *not* been kissed? To him, it was probably the natural climax to a pleasant day spent with a pretty girl. No more than that. It was foolish of her to attach any more importance to a perfectly everyday occurrence.

And yet – somehow, Tracy had had high hopes of her first kiss. Having waited for so long – for during the long years of her father's illness, all thoughts of romance had been put aside if, indeed, they had even occurred – she had felt obscurely that her first kiss would not be a simple, boy-girl event, a goodnight salute after a day out; but something that would shake her to the very roots of her soul, so that nothing afterwards could ever be quite the same again. And Nick's kisses, gentle and sweet as they were, more urgent and demanding as they had become, had left her feeling – slightly breathless perhaps, a little dazed from surprise, but nothing more. Certainly not shattered, or overwhelmed; certainly not shaken to the roots of her soul.

Sighing a little, Tracy realised that they were back at Belanice and climbing the steep, twisting road to the hotel. She realised all at once that she was aching with tiredness; that she was too exhausted to do any more than eat her dinner, sink into a deep, warm bath and then go to bed. So much had happened in the day; she needed time to relax, time to recall the various events and get them sorted out in her own mind.

It was only later, as she bathed after a sleepy goodnight to Nick at the door of her room, that Tracy noticed her wrist – and the bracelet of faint, purple bruises that encircled it.

For a moment, she stared incredulously – and then a warm blush crept over her body as she recalled the hard, almost cruel grasp of Iain Macalister's fingers as they sat, pressed close together on the bench in the riding hall of the Lipice Stud.

SIX

'If we walk along the other side of the lake,' Nick said, frowning at the map, 'we can meet the river and stay beside it all the way up to the waterfall. Marela says it is a real beauty spot, and people come from all over Slovenia to visit it.'

'Marela?'

'Yes, you know, that pretty girl at the

reception desk. I've managed to evolve my own brand of German to communicate with her. She's very helpful.'

'I'd have thought Melissa could have told you anything you needed to know,' Tracy remarked. 'She seems quite *au fait* with the area.'

'Goodness, I wouldn't dare ask Melissa – she terrifies me.' Nick widened his eyes in mock fear, so that Tracy laughed. 'She's too beautiful to be a courier – she ought to be a model or a film star or something. Anyway, she seems to be the exclusive property of the Macalister when not on duty. They were off again early this morning, did you notice?'

Tracy had noticed, but shook her head as if to imply that the doings of Melissa and 'the Macalister' were not nearly interesting enough to occupy her thoughts.

'Oh, yes, down to the village again. I noticed when I went down for some post-cards. Macalister seems to be uncommonly interested in some of the locals – but I suppose you hadn't noticed that, either? After all, he's not your favourite person, is he?'

'He certainly is not!' Tracy exclaimed. 'But why do you say he's interested in the locals?'

'Well, you remember seeing him and

Melissa in the village on Sunday. Talking to the old woman.' Tracy nodded. 'She was with them again this morning. Chattering away nineteen to the dozen. And that's another odd thing.' Nick stopped suddenly.

'What is? What's an odd thing?' Tracy forgot her resolve, made on the discovery of those faint bruises on her wrist, that from now on Iain Macalister was to be strictly avoided. She felt again the queer breathlessness that had assailed her as she stared at the marks, recalling the feel of his fingers, harsh as steel yet later oddly caressing. 'What's odd, Nick?'

'Well, it's not really odd, I suppose. Just that he speaks such good Yugoslavian – Serbo-Croat, or Slovenian, I don't know which. You'd think he'd spent half his life in the country. Yet I distinctly heard him telling that elderly couple – the Marchants – that he'd never been here before. Never been to Yugoslavia in his life.'

The walk beside the lake, under a warm sun that soon encouraged both Tracy and Nick to remove pullovers, was a pleasant respite from the long coach journey of the day before. Tracy decided that sitting in coaches was a waste of time, when one could be enjoying fresh air and sunshine together with as beautiful scenery as this. 'No more coach journeys,' she said.

'But what about the caves – you won't see them, if you don't go on any more coach trips. And they're worth seeing. And the trip into Italy – we must go on that.'

'I don't see why,' Tracy said. 'Why not use local transport? Much more fun – you're not jammed in with a lot of other tourists. Surely there's a bus service, or a train we could use?'

'You're a snob,' Nick told her teasingly; but he admitted that he had heard something about a daily bus service into the nearest Italian town. 'We'll find out about it tonight.'

Tracy smiled at him and made no answer to the accusation of being a snob. Perhaps she was; but she knew that the idea of travelling by local bus appealed to her far more than that of boarding a coach full of other sightseers. And it was not, she told herself sternly, simply because there would be less chance of having to travel with Iain Macalister and the beautiful Melissa. Yes – on the whole, she thought she probably *was* a snob! And pleased to stay that way, too!

They had come now to the end of the lake,

where there had at some time been a landslide. Rough stony scree reached right down to the bank and Tracy was thankful for her walking boots as she scrambled across. It was years since they had had such use – she and her father had done a good deal of walking in the Welsh hills at one time – but she had thought it a good idea to bring them to Yugoslavia with her. Now, looking at Nick's more conventional footwear, she was thankful to be wearing boots; it was too easy to twist an ankle in this kind of country.

Beside them, the rocks rose massively, ending in a steep slabby cliff far above. Tracy craned her neck to look at the great crags jutting against the sky. Across the lake she could see another mountain; less steep, clothed in skirts of fresh green beech and hazel which gave way to the darker colour of fir and conifer before reaching the snowline. At the summit glittered the windows of the ski-hotel and she could see, crawling up the last sheer faces of rock – the cable-car.

'We'll make that trip too, sometime,' Nick remarked, following the line of her gaze. 'You can get lunch at the top, and walk down. Make a good day out.'

'*Walk* down!' Tracy stared at the snow, dotted with fir trees, at the steep craggy rocks. 'I'm not walking down there! You couldn't.'

'Yes, you can. Look, the paths are marked on the map – they go around the back of those crags and down the valleys. There's probably not much snow there, and the paths are all well-marked, like this one along the lake.' Nick looked at her, his face alight with boyish excitement. 'You don't want to just come tamely down in a cable-car do you?'

Tracy thought that she did, but smiled at him and said no more. Nick really was very young, she thought fondly, a refreshing change after spending so many years out of young company. Immediately, she was washed with guilt, as if she had been deliberately comparing him with her father, to her father's detriment. But she had not really meant that; she was half-consciously aware, as perhaps previously she had not been, that a young person needs other young people at least part of the time. Nick, with his eagerness and unselfconscious enjoyment of life, seemed at times to be hardly more than a boy, yet Tracy judged him to be at least two or three years older than herself. It was merely her own pre-occupation with older people – her father,

Mr Osborne, even Aunt Chloe – that made him seem young by contrast, and herself older than he.

And then unbidden, there came into her mind the thought of Iain Macalister; stern, arrogant, hostile and unmistakably a good ten years older than herself. With him, she felt as childish and naïve as a ten-year-old. He was something quite outside her experience and left her, consequently, at a loss. Tracy stared at the blue, gently rippling waters of the lake, and pondered on this. With her father and Mr Osborne, she had been a person in her own right, and one to whom they looked for help, strength, support of one kind or another. With Nick, she was– Tracy shied away from all that she might be to Nick, but acknowledged that he looked on her as a friend, a companion, yet made her feel subtly older. But with Iain Macalister – well, with Iain Tracy was uncertain. She felt that he looked on her as a child, and a particularly annoying one at that; yet there had been in his eyes once or twice a look that spoke of something else; something that disturbed her queerly, something that she half feared yet half longed to know more deeply.

'Penny for them! Or should it be a *para*?'

Nick's voice broke in on her thoughts and Tracy jumped.

'Sorry! I was miles away. And my thoughts aren't worth even a *para*.' She smiled at him and began to walk along the narrow path again, leaving the lake behind and entering an airy conifer plantation. 'I'm not very good company, I'm afraid. Let's get on – we'll never get to the waterfall at this rate.'

Nick caught up with her and took her hand. They walked along in silence for a moment, then he said seriously, 'You're very good company, Tracy. I'm glad you came on this holiday too. I'd have been awfully lonely, without you to share things with.'

'Oh, there would have been someone,' Tracy said lightly.

'The sophisticated Melissa? I told you, she scares me! And there's no one else who would have wanted to spend their days like this, just wandering about and exploring. Can you see the Marchants or Mrs Andrews trailing around the lake – or me trailing around the shops with them?'

Tracy laughed and pointed out that if she had not come, her place would have undoubtedly been taken up by someone else.

'No one like you,' he said with sudden earnestness. 'There *isn't* anyone else like you!' And as Tracy could find no reply to this, they walked on in silence, hand in hand beneath the feathery branches of the firs, until they reached the village that lay at the foot of the mountain.

At this end of the lake, the mountains rose on all sides, for these were the first hills of the Julian Alps, spreading over into the other Alpine ranges and the Italian Dolomites. Tracy and Nick stood on the road among the little chalet-type houses with their steep wooden roofs, staring up at the great rocky walls which surrounded them. The whole aspect was wild, spectacular, breathtakingly beautiful – yet also rather oppressing. You could not, Tracy felt, live here without some of the character of that rugged, ruthless countryside becoming part of your own character; she saw the stern, forbidding implacability of the soaring cliffs reflected in the faces of the people they passed, although the leathery faces creased into smiles and their tentative greetings of 'Dobar Dan!' were returned. Still, if ever there were the need, she felt that the granite of the hills would show itself in the granite of unyielding tenacity, the obstinate courage that had been revealed by the Resistance during the last war.

Once more in the woods, they stopped by a spring and unpacked their lunch – laughing to find, again, the thick bread and generous portions of ham and cheese with which they had been regaled yesterday. However, Nick, on his foray to the shops that morning had augmented this with a slab of milk chocolate and a bottle of wine; and with apples and oranges to finish with, Tracy found the meal more than adequate.

They lay back in the shade of a large beech tree, listening to the sound of the spring, light and tinkling above the deeper roar of the river somewhere through the trees. Grasshoppers chirruped invisibly and somewhere a woodpecker tapped. And always, constantly, sounded the now-monotonous call of the cuckoos.

'You can understand why the Swiss use them so much in clocks,' Nick remarked, squinting up through half-closed eyes at the patch of blue that showed, shiftingly, through the branches of the trees. 'What I don't understand is why they bother to come on to England – the cuckoos, I mean, not the Swiss! – when this is on their way from Africa and just as good.'

Tracy did not feel disposed to argue about

natural history. She sat up, wrapping her arms round her knees, and looked thoughtfully down at Nick. Lying like that, his eyes almost shut, he looked younger than ever, his mouth soft as a child's, long brown lashes touching his cheeks.

'Where d'you live in London, Nick?' she asked, thinking how little they really knew about each other. 'Do you live alone?'

'No such luck.' He opened his eyes and grinned up at her. 'I live with my family. At Stanmore. Told you I'm a solicitor's clerk, didn't I? Well, I work with the firm my father's been with for years. I suppose he hopes I'll get to be a partner some day, but I doubt it. Too lazy.'

Tracy was slightly shocked. 'Oh, but you shouldn't be – I mean, work's important. You ought to get on, for your own sake.'

'Ought I?' Nick's eyes clouded a little, then he reached out for her hand. With the smile back in his voice, he said, 'No, Tracy, I'm not that sort... Too lazy to want to get on for my *own* sake. Now, if it were for someone *else's...*' His fingers caressed hers and Tracy knew a sudden moment of panic. She wished almost that she had not started this conversation; she wasn't ready yet for all its implications. Hastily, she withdrew her hand and began to pack the lunch things.

'Come on – we'll miss the waterfall,' she said breathlessly, and ridiculously. But at least it had the effect of diverting Nick's attention and making him laugh.

'They don't switch it off at five o'clock you know!' But he sat up and helped her with the lunch, packing the remains into his small rucksack and swinging it on to his back.

The path led them closer to the river, pouring ice-green and foaming down from the mountains. Tracy gazed at it, trying desperately to imprint it on her memory. Water, gushing, cascading water, foaming over rocks, almost yellow where the sun lit the slabs beneath it, opaquely green and shading to black under the rearing cliff – it was like a moving sculpture, flowing glass; a ballet as it danced, sending up little showers of spray. For centuries, she mused, water had swooped on that rock, just there, just so, so that it was now hollowed out smooth and round, the stream swirling in the rocky cup before rushing on. For centuries, the stream had gushed out of the mountain-side to hurl itself down here in its wild, torrential rush to meet the Danube and, later the sea.

'Tell you what,' Nick said; he had been studying the map as Tracy brooded. 'We needn't go the way everyone else does, over the bridge and up those steps – three hundred of them, Marela told me! There's an old path this side. We ought to be able to get right along the side of the cliff and see the fall from this side.'

'Will it be safe?' Tracy asked wondering whether she really wanted to see the waterfall from this side. 'I mean, if it's not used any more...'

'Oh, I expect it's quite all right. Probably it was easier to make the steps the other side, that's all. And if the path was on this side originally, doesn't that mean that this was the best view of it? Let's try it, anyway – we can always come back and go the other way if we want.' A few minutes later he exclaimed triumphantly, 'Yes – there it is, see? And the old way-marks are still there.' He pointed to the red and white 'bull's-eyes' which marked all the paths, painted on convenient rocks or trees. 'It's okay, Tracy.'

Tracy followed him up the steep, zig-zag path through the trees. Once again, she was abstracted. She realised now that she might have made a mistake in accepting Nick's company so readily, for several times she had encountered an intenseness in his gaze, a deepening of the frank admiration which she had first recognised, which disturbed her. She knew that she liked him immensely, felt comfortable and at ease with him. But she was afraid that he was soon going to ask more of her than mere liking, and she was not at all sure whether she could supply it.

The path was now levelling out and Nick, who was slightly ahead, stopped and let out a low whistle. He beckoned to Tracy and she hurried forward to join him.

They stood on the very edge of the cliff, high above the tumbling river. Two or three hundred feet below, the green water swirled in a chasm that at the bottom could have been scarcely a dozen feet wide. The grey slabs of rock were sprinkled with small trees and ferns which clung to the crevices, leaning out over the gorge; and above and beyond, the eye was led to a panorama of mountains glittering with snow, peak after peak stretching away into the far, far distance.

'Glad we came?' Nick murmured, his arm around Tracy's shoulders, and she nodded silently. There was a moment when neither of them spoke. Then Nick turned her, slowly and deliberately, to face him; and as their eyes met, his lips came down on hers in a long, gentle, yet searching kiss.

They drew apart and Tracy stared up into his eyes. She was slightly breathless, uncertain; she could feel the warm colour mounting her cheeks. And then, over his shoulder, she saw what before she had not had time to see; the waterfall, springing from the face of the cliff, a great spout of water, gushing in a ceaseless torrent from the grey wall of rock, pouring down in a white veil of spray to meet the churning, swirling pool below. And on the other side of the gorge, a little higher than their own path, was a small observation hut, roofed against the soaking mist of spray. A group of people stood within it, gazing at the fall.

But one of them was looking across the chasm, across the foaming river, directly at Nick and Tracy as they stood close together, Nick with his arms still about her slim body. That person stared straight into Tracy's eyes, his own glance as cold as the ice and snow on the mountains above, and she felt a chill crawl slowly down her spine. For a moment the beauty of the wild place, the sweetness and comfort of Nick's kiss, of his arms about her shoulders, dropped away, leaving only a bleakness and desolation such as one could imagine feeling if the very countryside had turned against one, with its implacability, its freezing severity.

It was, of course, Iain Macalister who watched them. And as Tracy stared back at him he turned deliberately away from her, put his own arm around the shoulders of the courier, Melissa, and led her out of the observation hut and away along the path, out of sight. And Tracy, watching them felt a sudden, inexplicable sense of loss and, hard on its heels, a furious resentment.

Suddenly, impulsively, Tracy turned to Nick and smiled into his eyes, delighting in the pleasure that she saw there.

'I *am* glad we came this way,' she whispered, 'It's very beautiful – and far, far better than climbing concrete steps on the other side!'

Dinner that night was served and eaten early, the chairs and tables being pushed back immediately everyone had finished, to form a half-circle around a large area of floor-space. Tracy, who had been looking forward to the folk-dancing display, smiled at Nick, who sat on her right, and at old Mrs Andrews on her left.

'The dancers have arrived already,' Mrs

123

Andrews volunteered. 'Young men and girls, all in national costume. Most colourful. I saw them go upstairs ten minutes ago.'

'And here they come again,' Nick observed. Tracy followed his glance and saw the dancers at the top of the stairs. She gave Nick a quick, smiling glance of pleasure, noticing that Iain Macalister sat on his other side; and with a sudden hardening of her heart, turned back to look at the dancers again, feeling that resentment at his presence – always watching her with that strange, brooding stare spoiling every moment of her precious, fragile relationship with Nick, making her feel a fool, a child – as if it were any of his business anyway!

At the end of the room stood a trio of musicians, with concertina, violin and pipe. They struck up a tune – a lilting, merry tune that made Tracy want to tap her own feet – and at once the dancers swung into action. The men, in their leather breeches, white shirts and feathered hats, swung the girls around, making the full skirts bell out beneath gaily coloured blouses. Tracy watched entranced as one man paraded solemnly between two lines of laughing, clapping dancers, a girl on each arm; laughed as a small, dark-haired girl chased the men with a broom; held her breath as another man, stocky and apple-cheeked, danced slowly in a circle, hands on hips and a large jug of beer on his head, gasped with delight as the prettiest girl of all appeared in a similar, but gayer dance, her head bearing a wide basket filled with scarlet carnations – the emblem of Slovenia.

The dancing lasted for over an hour, and Tracy took several photographs, thinking how Aunt Chloe would enjoy seeing the pictures. And then the musicians struck up again and the dancers were amongst the audience, choosing partners, grasping waists, pulling laughing, half-reluctant guests to their feet.

Tracy found herself in the arms of a tall, dark-eyed Yugoslav. She was being whirled around, lifted almost off her feet as he swung her in time to the music. Laughing, out of breath, she was passed on to another dancer – then another – and then, as the music quickened and the tempo of the dance became faster, more furious than ever, she felt a pair of strong arms about her, holding her tightly. She was pressed to a broad chest; warm breath touched her cheek. The music swelled to a crescendo. Tracy felt herself lifted into the air, swung so hard that her feet left the ground and she clung, laughing, to the man who held her so firmly. And then the tempo slowed, the music died away and the dance ended. Tracy, flushed and enchanted, recovered her balance as her partner set her gently back on her feet. She looked up to thank him – and froze.

Her eyes met a pair of chilling blue eyes lightened now by laughter yet still with splinters of ice lurking in their depth. For a moment she stared; then, a fury so intense that she dared not give it expression welling up within her, she turned on her heel and made for the door.

It was just outside that Nick found her a few minutes later. He held her for a few moments and Tracy rested against him, trying to control the shaking of her body. She had no idea what she could say to explain her behaviour; why, on discovering that her partner was none other than Iain Macalister, she should have reacted so violently. The very fact that she had actually enjoyed that short time in his arms – that the feel of them about her, so different from other arms which had held her during the dance, had seemed somehow *right* – had intensified her reaction. But how she could explain this to Nick, she had no idea.

And then she found that there was, thankfully, no need to. For Nick's arms were about her, his lips in her hair and he was murmuring soft endearments. Tracy, her trembling slowly coming to an end, listened in bewilderment. He was saying that he loved her – that he couldn't live without her – that she must be his, now and always. He was asking her to marry him!

'Marry you?' she repeated, as if the words were in a foreign language. 'But we've only known each other a few days.'

'What does that matter? A few hours, a few days, a few years – Tracy, what does *time* matter? I knew in the first few minutes! And we'll have all the rest of our lives to get to know each other – if only you'll say yes! Tracy?'

'I – I don't know.' She was too shaken to think clearly. She knew in her heart that she should have foreseen this – indeed, *had* foreseen it, for she had known as they stood watching the waterfall that Nick was, or at least believed himself to be falling in love with her. But, wanting only to enjoy the beauty of the place and recover a little from the emotional trauma of the past few months, she had refused to acknowledge the fact, preferring to divert all Nick's attempts to tell her. Now, because of her foolish behaviour over Iain, the moment had crept up on her unawares. Nick had proposed marriage. He was entitled to an answer.

'Please, Tracy,' he murmured, his lips gentle on her cheek. 'I'd be good to you, I swear. We'd have a happy life. And I'd work hard – I wouldn't be lazy, with a wife like you to work for!'

Tracy stared past his shoulder at the dark silhouette of the mountains against the paler sky. The moon was just climbing into view, a thin crescent, sharp and bright. She thought of being married to Nick; living in a little house in Stanmore, far away from Herefordshire and her old life. A completely new start. The idea caused a pang in her heart – but would it be such a bad thing? And Nick *would* be good to her – she was sure of that. He would adore her, work for her. They enjoyed each other's company, she felt at ease with him. Could that be love?

'Say yes, Tracy,' Nick whispered again, and suddenly she made up her mind.

'Yes, Nick,' she whispered back. 'But – please let's keep it a secret just for a while, shall we? Just between ourselves – till I get used to the idea.'

His arms and lips told her his joy, and then he said in a low tone. 'I want to shout it from the housetops, Tracy – but if that's how you want it. Just for a while. Just until we go home, all right?'

Tracy nodded, trying to quell a niggling feeling that she, too, should be feeling as joyful as Nick. But perhaps her own emotions had been numbed; after a while, when the full happiness of it all blossomed within her, she would remember this night, with the crescent moon rising over the mountains and the sound of gay Yugoslavian folk music lilting behind her, as a night of magical enchantment.

'Nick,' she said, overcome with weariness, 'Can we say goodnight now? I'm almost asleep on my feet – I'm sorry!'

And it was only a short time later, when Tracy was lying in bed, bemused, her mind a whirling confusion of rushing waterfalls, foaming rivers, crescent moons and Nick's gentle kisses, that she found herself suddenly comparing two pairs of arms – Nick's tender and caressing as they held her, and another pair, hard and strong as steel bands, which gripped her body and swung her off her feet, which seemed to own and command her, leaving her no will of her own...

Impatiently, angrily, Tracy turned over and thumped her pillow. Five minutes later, she was fast asleep.

SEVEN

Italy, Tracy decided, was quite different from Yugoslavia even though Belanice and the little Italian market-town of Terrisio were little more than a dozen miles apart. She gazed around her with delighted eyes as she and Nick disembarked from the local bus – a surprisingly modern and luxurious motor-coach – which had brought them across the border that morning.

The journey itself had been, as Tracy had prophesied, an entertainment in itself. There had been an hilarious exchange between Nick and the Yugoslavian conductor who – she suspected – had known very well where they wanted to go, but had pretended complete lack of understanding. Eventually, amid much laughter and badinage from other passengers, he had

130

taken their fares and given them tickets, impressing on them in a mixture of bad German and sign language, that they must have lira for the return fare.

'How lovely!' Tracy exclaimed when Nick explained this to her. 'One currency to go and another to come back! I suppose that's because they take the fares in those particular countries. But suppose he didn't take our fare until we are back across the border – would it be dinars or lira?'

'Too complicated for me,' Nick answered. 'We'll just have to make sure we've got the right amount of lira for our fare back! Did you remember your passport?'

'Of course.' Tracy had carried it with her wherever she went each day of the holiday, but checked now to make sure it really was in her bag. 'I must say, it seems odd to have to take a passport to go shopping twelve miles away!' It all added to the fun however, and she was suitably awed by the Customs post and the uniformed men who walked down the coach, glancing to left and right as they went.

Terrisio was a small town with a long main street and two or three lesser shopping streets. They entered it over an old bridge, crossing a deep gorge with a green river at

131

its bottom. The houses of Terrisio climbed up the steep sides of a hill, and above them Tracy could see the onion-shaped dome of a church.

The coach swerved into the town, passing shops and houses that looked as if they were ready for a carnival. Tracy stared at the window-boxes high on the walls, gay with flowers; at the shops with huge displays of baskets, wine and souvenirs outside on the pavements; at *trattoria* with chairs and tables under gay umbrellas. Signs and notices clustered on the walls, jostling for the best position; and shoppers thronged the streets, ignoring the traffic so that the coach-driver had his work cut out to avoid running them down.

'Well, here we are in Italy.' Nick took her hand as she climbed down from the coach. 'Bit different from Belanice, isn't it?'

'It's so noisy – and lively!' Tracy immediately felt guilty and added hastily. 'I love Belanice, of course, it's so peaceful and beautiful. But this – well, as you say, it certainly is different!'

Terrisio was bursting with noisy, laughing, chattering life, and Tracy found herself caught up in it at once. Hand in hand, she and Nick joined the crowds, explored the

crowded shops bursting with colourful souvenirs, gazed up at peeling, ornate house-
fronts. They bought ice-cream, wide-eyed as
children to see different coloured ices piled
on top of each other in cornets; blinked at
baskets full of wines at prices which would
surely scarcely have covered the cost of the
bottles; admired huge glossy tomatoes and
cherries and puzzled over public notices.

'How strange that it should all be so
different only a few miles away,' Tracy said
thoughtfully. 'Yugoslavia's lovely – beautiful
– and the people are nice. But they haven't
got this – exuberance, this colour.'

'I know what you mean,' Nick nodded.
'The streets are bare and plain, compared to
these – no notices, hardly any advertise-
ments. And the shops don't have anything
like the amount of things in them.'

'They seem more serious about life – perhaps they just like to live simply.' Tracy
paused, looking up at a huge bunch of
coloured balls. 'It's rather like Wales in some
ways – you can see the real thing, the true
beauty with no trappings. I think it would
wear me out to live with all this bustle and
noise, none of it really meaning very much.
I'm afraid I'm just a simple country girl,
Nick – I like a quiet life!'

Nick glanced down at her, his eyes amused and twinkling. 'Just wait till you get to Stanmore!' he advised. '*Then* you'll see some real life – why, it makes all this seem like a nursery playgroup!' And Tracy laughed with him, aware that she was being teased and not in the least upset about it.

'By the way,' Nick remarked as they walked hand in hand along the crowded street. 'Your boy-friend was about early again today.'

'My – who? My *boy*-friend?'

'The Highland Chief. Macalister. Down in the village with the old woman.' Nick lifted her left hand looking at the third finger and rubbed it gently with his thumb. 'You know, Tracy, I wish you'd let us make our engagement official. I'd quite like to warn him off!'

'Warn him off?' Tracy stared at him, her face hot. 'Nick Lester, what are you talking about? Warn off Iain Macalister? I've told you before, he has no interest in me nor I in him! Don't tell me you're going to be jealous of every man I meet – because I couldn't stand that!'

'Hey, steady on! Of course I'm not jealous – I'm the faithful and trusting type, don't you know that? But if you think Iain

Macalister has no interest in you, you're sadly wrong. He most certainly has – why, he never takes his eyes off you! And I don't want to warn him off because I'm jealous – no, it gives me quite a thrill to think that my girl's so attractive. I want to warn him off for *your* sake, my dear silly love – because I'd got more than an idea that you don't return his interest.'

'Oh.' Tracy felt deflated. 'Oh, all right. I'm sorry, Nick.' And because she seemed once again to have made a fool of herself, she turned quickly to the nearest shop window and said brightly, 'Oh, look, what lovely things.'

And then she wished that she hadn't. For the shop was a jeweller's, its window full of rings; and Nick, stopping and drawing her close to his side, said seriously, 'Yes – they are lovely things. Oh, Tracy, forget all this secrecy nonsense – let me buy you a ring now. An engagement ring!'

Tracy stared at the rings. Once again, her mind was confused, muddled. One part of it urged her to accept – after all, she had already accepted Nick's proposal, hadn't she? So why not make it public? Why not wear his ring, wear it with pride and happiness just as a newly-engaged girl should?

What was preventing her from taking this final step?

She only knew that it had something to do with Iain Macalister. That something in his ice-cold eyes – some hint of mockery on catching sight of an engagement ring on her finger – could turn the whole thing sour, spoil the happiness for both herself and for Nick. Why it should be, she could not imagine – but she longed to get back to England, away from that icy gaze, away from the hostility that invariably sprang up between them, before announcing to the world her intention to marry Nick Lester.

She was aware suddenly of Nick's face – an almost comical mixture of pleading and despair – and forgot her own problems, asking half-laughingly what was wrong.

'Money!' he said mournfully. 'Here I am, offering to buy you an engagement ring – and I've only got a few pounds on me. Not enough for what I'd like to get you, and no chance of more until we get back to London. I'm sorry, Tracy.'

'Don't worry,' she said quickly, relief spreading through her. 'I really would rather wait.' And when they were back in London, she could forget the arrogant Scot whose face came so often between her and Nick, whose blue eyes disturbed her so.

'Still, it would have been fun...' Nick brightened. 'Tell you what – we *will* buy a ring, Tracy. Just a little one, a plain one. Just for now. And you can wear it when we're together – put it on another finger when other people are about if you like. How about that?' He was boyish, eager again, and Tracy could not help laughing. She couldn't refuse this, and they went into the shop, hand in hand, and giggling like children.

The Italian shopkeeper brightened at once. He gazed at them paternally, sentimentally, held out his own hands to welcome them in. It was clear that he knew exactly what they wanted; and although he spoke no English, and neither Tracy nor Nick had any idea of Italian, he went at once to the window and brought in a tray of rings.

'No, no,' Nick said, waving his hand dismissively. 'Too expensive.' He pulled out his wallet. 'Not much money.'

The Italian hardly showed his disappointment. He brought a tray of cheaper rings for their examination; then another, and another. Soon he and Nick were bending over them eagerly, each picking out rings and trying them on Tracy's fingers, until, laughing helplessly, she protested.

'Look, *I'd* like to have a say too!' She bent over the tray of rings; then, after a long look, picked out one with a single blue stone in it, the gold worked around the stone in an intricate design. She slid it on to her finger. It fitted perfectly.

'That's the one,' Tracy said firmly; and although Nick said it was too plain, too inexpensive, she stayed firm. 'It will be a lovely souvenir of our holiday,' she told him. 'Really, Nick, it *is* the one I like best.'

'Then that's all that matters,' he answered; and, accompanied by many good wishes – unfortunately all quite incomprehensible – from the shopkeeper, they went out again into the street.

The ring felt strange on Tracy's finger, and she kept glancing at it, unable to believe what it really meant. It was inconceivable that she had really agreed to marry this eager young man, whom she had only known for a few days. But she had, his proud, possessive expression told her that; that and the way he held her hand, touching the ring himself every now and then as if to make sure that it was really there.

And then they arrived at the open-air market and all solemnity vanished as they explored, shrugging off the blandishments of stall-holders, examining the sweaters, belts, coats and gadgets that were for sale. Tracy bought a bag of cherries, discovering that any currency was acceptable in this strange, fairground of a town. She paid in Yugoslavian dinars and received change in lira – enough they discovered after considerable counting and calculation, to get them back to Belanice on the bus.

'I'll put that away separately, then we don't have to worry any more,' she smiled. And then, 'Goodness, is that the time?'

'It's gone two,' Nick said. 'Oh – but time's an hour different here, isn't it! Anyway, my stomach says it's lunchtime – shall we try one of the *trattoria*?'

They swung up the hill and into a café, rejoicing in the very Italian look of the linoleum-covered tables, the plump smiling waitress who came forward to welcome them. It seemed, Tracy thought happily, that everything was on their side today. She sat and gazed at her ring, thinking that perhaps after all she would keep it on; and only half-heard Nick when he asked what she would like to eat.

'Spaghetti?' the waitress asked, beaming. 'Cannelloni? Lasagna?'

'Oh – lasagna, please.' It was lucky that one already knew so many Italian words. And she sat wrapped in a pleasant dream until the lasagna came; a dream that Nick, holding her hand closely in his, seemed to have no wish to interrupt; perhaps he was sharing it.

The rest of the day passed in an equally dreamlike state. It seemed to Tracy that childhood had returned; that the cares that had beset her for, almost, as long as she could remember, had at last been thrown aside for a new world of carefree rapture – wasn't there a quotation or something about that, she wondered vaguely. It didn't really matter though; all that mattered was that when she returned to England, there would be no need to return to her old life, to a cottage full of memories – to an elderly author and his researches. To an empty future.

Instead, she would be returning to wedding plans, to house-hunting with Nick, to a family who he assured her would love her as much as he did. A sister, the same age as herself, a younger brother, parents who took life easily and didn't impose fetters – yes, Tracy would have guessed his family would be like that.

And if, at times, the thought of blue eyes, cold and lonely – and why should that adjective come to mind? – disturbed her dreams, Tracy pushed them firmly away. Iain Macalister, she told herself fiercely, yet again, was nothing to her; nor she to him.

It was something of a disappointment, after the golden day, to find Nick definitely seedy next day, and unwilling to go out at all. It must, he told Tracy as he toyed miserably with a late breakfast, have been the ice-cream he had eaten after lunch – Tracy had had a fruit salad. He would stay in today and probably be better tomorrow.

'Don't you hang about,' he said, 'I'll go back to bed. You go and explore somewhere – only, take care. And wear our ring!'

Tracy smiled at him and promised to take care, and to wear the ring. She thought that he was probably already on the way to recovery and needed only a good rest, perhaps a long sleep, to be perfectly all right again. Missing him a little, for they had spent so much of their time together during the past few days, she set off down the hill towards the lake.

She had not arranged to take a packed lunch and decided to spend the morning in the village, then to take a walk along one of the mountain tracks in the afternoon. Accordingly, she wandered into the narrow village streets, enjoying the warmth of the sun on her head, and greeting the villagers with a friendly 'Dobar Dan.'

It was a warm, sunny morning and Tracy found herself reluctant to go back to the hotel for lunch. Nick would almost certainly stay in bed, unaware of whether she returned or not, so would be unlikely to miss her. There seemed to be little point in climbing up the steep knoll merely to come down again in the afternoon; and a sudden longing to explore the gorge again, and perhaps go further up the valley, possessed her. After some hesitation, she decided to go into the small supermarket and buy something for a snack.

She bought some cheese, rolls and a couple of bananas, with a foil container of fruit juice to drink; these containers, complete with straw, were popular with everyone, she noticed, and were easy to carry. She packed the food into her small nylon rucksack and slipped it on to her shoulders.

'Dobar Dan!' It was an old woman, watching her with friendly black eyes; and with some surprise Tracy recognised the woman she had seen with Iain Macalister the other day. She smiled back, wondering whether the woman spoke English, but her tentative enquiry was met with a shake of her head. Shrugging helplessly, they both laughed and Tracy turned to walk on along the street.

It was strange, this interest of Iain's in the local people. Strange too the way the old woman had evidently welcomed him into her home – like an old friend, almost. And yet someone had told her – was it Nick? – that Iain had never been to Yugoslavia before. Why, then, should he be immediately acquainted with the people of the village, visiting them in their homes less then twenty-four hours after his arrival? Why was he able to speak the language so fluently?

It was somewhat disquieting, although why it should be Tracy found it hard to explain, even to herself. Perhaps it was just the slightly bizarre event of his knowing a language that was uncommon in England. Tracy shook herself mentally; probably there was some quite rational explanation, such as his knowing a Yugoslavian at home who had taught him the language. He might even have learned it from records!

Smiling at the thought of Iain Macalister

earnestly listening to language records, Tracy left the village and walked steadily on along the track leading to the gorge. She was on the side of the hill now, above Belanice, and paused to look back. The great lake shimmered in the morning sun, the village clustered around the bridge at the end. Somewhere on the other side was the hotel – with, Tracy thought with a guilty pang at having forgotten him so quickly, Nick inside it. And beyond the hotel were the mountains, the nearest one with its ski hotel twinkling at the top, the snowy peaks stretching out behind it.

The gorge was as beautiful and evocative as it had been on their first visit. Tracy chose a spot where she could sit on a rock and watch the tumbling water. She drew her knees up to her chin, wrapped her arms round her legs and gazed down.

She had been right to come alone, she thought dreamily. The magic of the place had touched her when she was here with Nick, but because it had not touched him too, it had retreated. Now it was on her, in a flood as full as that of the foaming water below. She was lost in a world of surging, eddying movement, a maelstrom of dizzying noise, the thunder of water against rock filling her ears, filling her head, driving out all thought so that she was completely and truly care-free for the first time in years.

How long she sat there, she had no idea. It was only slowly that the magic receded, leaving her relaxed and calm. And it was then, as she lifted her head and glanced bemusedly around, unsure at first as to where she was, that she realised that she was not alone.

Iain Macalister sat on a rock nearby. He was perfectly still, one leg slightly drawn up so that his arm could rest casually across it; and he was watching her.

Tracy gazed back at him. It was as if all movement had stopped. For a few moments, she was unaware of birds calling, of grasshoppers chirruping, even of the ceaseless roar of the water below. She gazed at Iain Macalister and he at her, and she knew only that the magic of the place was undiminished by his presence; that all their hostility had disappeared as if washed away.

'You've been a long way away, Tracy,' he said at last, and Tracy realised that this was the first time he had used her name. He got up and came over to her, looking down unsmilingly; but there was no ice in his eyes now. 'It's a very strange place, this. Come.'

And he stretched out his hand.

Tracy got up. She did not take the hand he offered, but when he turned she turned with him and they walked, side by side, not speaking. They were in the trees now, and the sun poked long fingers down to touch the forget-me-nots and lilies-of-the-valley that carpeted the ground. Somewhere, a cuckoo called; and somewhere else, another answered it.

'How long were you watching me?' Tracy asked presently.

'I don't know. Time stopped.' He glanced at his watch. 'It's nearly one. Did you bring any lunch?'

Tracy indicated her scarlet rucksack.

'Good. So there's no hurry.' He looked down at her, oddly different. 'You don't mind us taking this path together?'

And Tracy, still in her odd, dreamlike state, shook her head. On this day, she felt, she could cope with anything and anyone – even Iain Macalister.

Not that he seemed to need much coping with. They walked side by side, not touching each other, hardly speaking. It was as if he was a different man – as if they were both different people. Yet Tracy was aware of a communication between them, unspoken

146

but strangely satisfying. She had felt it when they sat together at Lipice, watching the ballet of the white horses. She felt it again now as they strolled beside a rushing mountain stream under the Yugoslavian sky.

By unspoken consent they left the stream, crossing an old stone bridge that could have come straight from a fairytale. Tracy leaned over its parapet, gazing down into the clear water, and felt Iain's hand laid restrainingly on her shoulder.

'The parapet doesn't look too safe to me,' he said as she turned and he took his hand away. Tracy smiled at him, but could not speak. The feel of his hand still burned through the thin cotton of her shirt, and she was oddly shaken.

The track led on, up through more trees – conifers, dark and mysterious. Still, below on their right, they could hear the sound of the water, but it was muted now, softened by the thick growth between them. They passed clearings in the forest where trees had been felled; some of them were piled up ready for collection, some still lay strewn on the forest floor, their trunks smooth and pale where the rough bark had been stripped off.

And then the track came to the top of the

hill, and Tracy cried out with delight.

They were standing on the rim of a vast bowl. Ahead, and all around, were mountains – vast and jagged, rearing fantastically towards the sky. And below, cupped in the ring of grey rock, lay a wide green valley, perfect in its contrast. The river ran like a silvered ribbon through the bright green grass. Here and there were dotted bushes, shrubs and small trees; and in between them stood the small wooden buildings that looked like tiny cottages and were, Tracy knew, known as 'dairymen's huts' and were stuffed with hay for the cattle.

High overhead two raven flew, their voices harsh as if the rocks themselves spoke. A flock of Nubian goats, long spaniel ears flopping, grazed nearby. But nothing else moved. It was as if Tracy and Iain had the world to themselves.

'Lunch down there, I think lassie,' Iain said at last, and they went on down the track until they could cross the lush grass to the stream. Tracy slipped off her rucksack and knelt to bathe her face.

'It's icy!' she exclaimed, laughing and Iain smiled suddenly, his sombre face breaking into laughter.

'It's straight off the mountain snow.' He

dropped his own rucksack on the grass and Tracy cried out.

'Put it on a rock – you'll hurt the flowers. Look.' She cupped her hand beside them. 'Lilies-of-the-valley – I've never seen so many. And these lovely blue gentians – and these are Soloman's Seal. I don't know what all the others are.'

They shared their lunch, laughing at Iain's provisions – 'ham and cheese *again*!' – and enjoying Tracy's fruit juice mixed with his bottle of mineral water. Afterwards, they lay back among the flowers, staring up at the wheeling mountains above, enclosed in their own private world; and once again it was as if Time had stopped.

And then Tracy was aware of Iain raising himself on his elbow, staring down at her. She gazed up into the intense blue eyes, her own widening. Her heart jerked against her ribs and her mouth went suddenly dry as she remembered – and wondered how she had ever forgotten – this man's extreme hostility towards her; his arrogance, his rudeness. What was she doing alone here, with him? How could she ever have allowed herself to–

Her thoughts stopped abruptly as his head came down to hers; and when he drew away her face was burning, her eyes closed against the watching mountains, her heart bounding like a running deer.

'Don't,' she whispered faintly; and then again, after a moment, 'Don't!'

'Why not?' he murmured, his voice rough-edged. 'Tell me – why not?'

Bemused, weakened, Tracy clung to what remained of her strength. 'Because I – because we – you don't – I don't *want* you to!' she finished desperately, and saw laughter in his eyes. And then, angrily, 'And if I don't want to, that should be reason enough!'

'Surely,' he agreed, his eyes glinting. 'But are you sure it's true?'

Tracy stared at him for a full minute. Then, her face flaming, she sat up; knelt in the grass, bruising the flowers, and said with as much ice in her voice as she could muster, 'Oh, yes, Mr Macalister – I'm quite sure it's true. You see, I'm not the sort of girl to enjoy kissing men I don't really like – or men who I don't really care much about. And since I have a perfectly good fiancé of my own – well, I don't really need to indulge in idle dalli–'

'Fiancé?' His face darkened. He shot out a hand, grasped her wrist. 'You've no ring –

150

what do you mean?'

'I do have a ring!' Tracy held out her right hand, with its blue stone on the third finger. *This* is my ring. It's on my right hand – because – because–' she floundered, then recovered herself– '–because it's a little loose on my left and I don't want to lose it. But since you don't seem to believe me, I'll put it on my left hand – there! *Now* are you satisfied?'

Iain stared at the ring, his expression unreadable. At last he took his eyes from it and looked into Tracy's face. She stared back, flinching a little. His gaze searched hers, as if he would find some truth there. And then, with a heavy sigh, he turned away, looking into the mountains, his face shuttered and remote.

'Satisfied?' he said, in a tone so low that Tracy was scarcely sure she heard him. 'I wouldn't say that *satisfied* was the right word. But yes – I believe you. If that's what you want.' He paused and then said, his voice flat. 'I suppose it's young Lester.'

'Nick – yes, it is.'

'So why are you out with me?'

'I'm not "out with you",' Tracy said cruelly. 'We just happened to be going the same way.' She ignored the pang that his

151

expression caused her and went on determinedly. 'Nick's not very well today, or of course we'd be together.'

'I'm surprised you aren't beside him, doing the ministering angel act,' Iain said with bitterness. 'You know – holding the frail hand, mopping the fevered brow. But that wouldn't really be your scene, would it? I should think you'd steer clear of the sickroom – rather be out in the sunshine, like the butterfly you are, flitting to a new flower. It takes a stronger personality to look after the sick and suffering–'

Tracy leapt to her feet. She began hastily to repack her rucksack. She could think of nothing except her urgent need to get away from this man, away from the valley that had seemed so enchanted and was now like a prison, trapping her with its menacing grey walls of rock and mountains. Fumbling, half-blinded by the tears, she groped at the straps and then felt Iain's hand once more on her wrist.

'All right – that was going a bit too far and I'm sorry,' he said more quietly. 'But you can hardly blame me for calling you a butterfly. You weren't engaged to young Lester when you came out here – in fact, I suspect you only met him on the day we left

England. Yet here you are, engaged to him – yet spending a day in a lonely valley with me – with a strange man of whom you know nothing.' Gripping her wrists, he forced her round to face him and stared down into her eyes, his own hard and angry. 'You are a butterfly, Tracy Pelham,' he said softly, 'and you ask for all you get.' His face drew nearer. 'And before you leave this valley, you are going to know what you're missing – getting yourself engaged to a mere boy. You're going to be kissed – at least once in your life – by a real man!'

Like lightning, his hands left her wrists; but before Tracy could twist away, his arms were round her, holding her like bands of steel. For the third time his lips met hers, hard, demanding, drawing a response so involuntary that Tracy gasped, feeling her limbs weaken; and when he let her go, she staggered.

'Now you can go,' he said, and his voice shook as Tracy turned blindly away from him. She picked up her rucksack and heaved it on to her shoulders. Then, without looking back, she walked away from him, away up the mountain track towards the rim of the valley.

At the top, she turned. The ravens still flew

amongst the high crags; the goats still browsed in the lush grass. And, close to the glittering mountain stream that rushed ever towards the gorge, sat Iain Macalister. His hard, muscular body, which Tracy could still feel pressed against her own, was made small by the distance. He looked very lonely, sitting there in that vast landscape; lonely and again, as he had seemed for a moment in Lipice, vulnerable.

Tracy repressed a sudden insane desire to rush back to him, to throw herself into those powerful arms, to raise her face to his to kiss and be kissed. And then, with a rush of horror, she knew the truth. She knew, and for the first time faced, that she had been attracted to Iain Macalister ever since she had first seen him, mopping furiously at his suit in the airport lounge. She knew that he too was attracted to her, that one day the attraction might be acknowledged. But against that had been her fear of getting involved, her bruised emotions shying away from the possibility of fresh hurt. She had taken refuge in the peace of Nick's uncomplicated friendship, subconsciously aware that with him she was unlikely to feel deeply and so would not run any risk of pain.

Her unacknowledged plans for defence

had backfired, she thought ruefully as she turned away from the valley and made her way slowly back to the gorge. Now she was engaged to Nick – whom, she realised at last, she did not love – and had finally, irrevocably, quarrelled with Iain. And she knew, with a sudden stab of real misery, that when Iain had kissed her he had touched depths of emotion she had never known before. Depths – she felt a sob rising in her throat – that she would never, now, know again.

Tracy wandered back beside the gorge, her head filled again with the sound of the rushing, roaring water that tumbled beneath. But now the magic was gone and her face was wet with tears for what she had lost.

EIGHT

The rest of the day passed somehow. It was mid-afternoon when Tracy returned to the hotel. Nick was nowhere to be seen and she deduced that he was still in bed. She was thankful for this; her mind and emotions were in such turmoil that to have had to meet him just then would have been more than she could bear. She went to her own room, showered, and lay on the bed, staring at the ceiling.

She knew now she loved Iain Macalister – loved him desperately, deeply and irrevocably. And she knew that, whatever his feelings about her – and she felt sure that they were nothing more than a passing attraction, a desire to conquer – there was now no chance of his ever returning that love. No chance of her ever knowing again the joy of a true bond, the unspoken communication that had been between them both at Lipice and this afternoon by the gorge. For a short time, she had known what it was to share magic; now, it was lost for ever. For it had never existed between herself and Nick.

With a deep sigh, Tracy turned her mind to Nick. What was she to do, to say? Only two days ago, standing outside the hotel and watching a crescent moon rise over the mountain, she had promised to marry him. She had looked forward to going home with him, to meeting his family, starting a new life. Now, she was sharply aware that this was impossible; that whatever she did now was going to result in pain, for herself and for Nick – most of all for Nick, who had done nothing to deserve it. She thought of those merry brown eyes dimmed with pain, the boyish grin gone from the mobile mouth to leave it soured with disappointment – and she groaned.

'...so we wondered if you would like to join us,' Mrs Marchant finished eagerly. 'After all, if there is room for four in the car, it seems a pity only to use two of the seats. And we've both noticed how you and your young man seem to love the countryside. With a car, one can go where one likes.'

'Yes,' Tracy glanced at Nick. She had come down to dinner fully intending to break their engagement – as gently as possible, of course, but she felt unable to continue with what had become a pathetic lie. But as soon as she had arrived in the dining-room, pleased to see that he was well enough to face the meal, Mrs Marchant had left her own seat and hurried over.

The proposition was that she and Nick should share a car which the Marchants were hiring next day. They had, Mrs Marchant explained, intended going with Mrs Andrews and her companion; but Mrs

Andrews had a migraine and would not be up to it for two days at least.

'So as the car has already been booked, we have to have it,' Mrs Marchant told Tracy. 'Do say you'll come.'

Nick caught her doubtful glance and smiled reassuringly. 'It's O.K. Tracy – I feel a lot better now. I'll be right as rain tomorrow, and I must say a car ride will probably suit me better than walking.' He turned to Mrs Marchant. 'Of course we'll come – and thanks for thinking of us.'

Tracy ate her dinner silently. She was beginning to see the utter impossibility of talking seriously to Nick now. How *could* she tell him that his dreams were over, that she could not marry him? How could she spoil his happiness, ruin his holiday he had obviously looked forward to? She sighed and laid down her spoon.

'You're all right, darling, aren't you?' Nick said anxiously. 'Not feeling groggy? Tell me what you've been doing today.'

And that was impossible too. Tracy folded up her napkin and smiled wanly.

'Sorry, Nick – I've got a bit of a headache. I'll go to bed early, I think.'

'But you'll be all right tomorrow?' He reached across the table and clasped her hand. 'I'm looking forward to this trip, Tracy. Mr Marchant suggested we go along a track that leads right up to the foot of the Triglav – the highest mountain in Yugoslavia. It'll be terrific scenery – and marvellous with you to share it.' He gazed at her, his brown eyes soft with love. 'You go to bed now, and have a good sleep. There'll be no hurry tomorrow – and we'll manage to snatch a bit of time to ourselves, too.'

Tracy sat for a long time on her balcony, looking out over the dark lake. The moon was just rising when she finally got up to go to bed; no longer a thin, bright edge but a sturdy crescent, swelling with each night. It had scarcely been born when she met Nick and Iain on that first day. What would have happened before it faded again to darkness; where would they all be, with their torn emotions and bruised hearts?

'From this village,' Mr Marchant said, studying the map, 'we just keep straight on up the track until we reach the mountain hut. That's nearly at the foot of the mountain – we should have a good view from there. You can walk further on, if you like, to reach the face itself.'

'We'll leave that to you youngsters,' Mrs

Marchant smiled, and Nick squeezed Tracy's hand.

Tracy leaned forward to peer out of the car window. The village was quite a large one; neat and modern, with a large area of grass, a school and two or three shops amongst the modern houses. She liked the Scandinavian style of building, with its steep roofs and balconies at all the upstairs windows. Winding down the window, she could hear the sound of children's voices from the school; they were singing, laughing. Ahead, the skyline was broken by the now-familiar sight of jagged peaks and grey, rugged mountains. But these were the mountains of the Triglav range, highest and most cruel in the whole of Yugoslavia. There was something sombre about them, and Tracy shivered a little.

Mr Marchant started the car again and they went on up the village street. They had stopped for coffee at the inevitable café, having been travelling for nearly two hours; now they were leaving behind the last few houses of the village, the road rough beneath the wheels as it rose gradually into the wilder forests of the mountains.

'Look at that!' Mrs Marchant exclaimed, pointing up the valley, and they gazed in awe. Ahead, the peaks formed a barrier; to their left a great wall of rock towered over them, its face too harsh and steep even for a fir tree to grow. Beneath it and beside the road ran the river, foaming over the rocks, clear and green as all the mountain rivers were. To their right the forest stretched dark and impenetrable.

'You can certainly believe that wolves and bears might live here – as the books say they do.' Mr Marchant remarked. 'I don't think I'd want to wander far in these woods alone – especially as night came on!'

'It's rather a Canadian type of scenery,' his wife remarked. 'Very beautiful. Let's get out and take some photos, Jim.'

Nick and Tracy wandered a short way off and Nick looked at her anxiously.

'I've hardly had a moment to talk to you today,' he said. 'You are feeling better, aren't you? You still look a bit pale.'

'I'm all right. It's just – well, so much as happened so quickly. I suppose I'm a bit overwhelmed.' She smiled at him, knowing that that was not what she meant to say at all. But there was no chance of serious conversation with the Marchants so near; and she couldn't break her news here. The scenery was too tremendous, too *important* for human woes. How many other little dreams had been enacted beneath the lowering mountains, she wondered; and how many were forgotten now, as if they had never been?

Nick, however, was beset by no such doubts. He drew her into the shadow of the trees and kissed her. 'Dear Tracy. Dear, darling sweet Tracy.' He kissed her again. 'I don't know why we agreed to come, do you? I'd far rather be on our own.'

Flustered, Tracy pulled away a little, then relented as she caught the hurt in his eyes. 'Sorry, Nick – I thought I heard Mrs Marchant calling...' She turned away, miserably conscious that, sweet as she had found Nick's kisses before, their sweetness had been spoiled by the harsh, demanding passion of Iain Macalister's lips. She knew now what he had meant by the difference between the kisses of a man and a boy. And Nick – cheerful, devoted Nick – *was* still a boy.

Still silent, and aware of Nick's puzzled, slightly hurt glance, Tracy climbed back into the car. The Marchants, their photographing done, were there already and Mr Marchant let in the clutch. Slowly, the car moved on up the track.

As they drove deeper into the mountains, climbing steadily all the time, the scenery became wilder and even more spectacular. Tracy forgot her troubles and gazed out, revelling in the sheer untamability of it all. Here, no development could ever change things; no estate could be built, no intensive farming take place. There would be no ugly buildings to mar the beauty, no great factories, no sprawling urbanisation. Here, the country was as it had always been; and man was, as she had felt before, a mere fly to be brushed from its face; helpless in the face of nature.

'Makes you feel insignificant, doesn't it?' Nick said, surprising her.

'Some people don't like it for that very reason.' Mr Marchant remarked. 'Gives their ego a nasty shock! Hallo – I thought we'd left human habitation behind!'

The track was curving to the right. High above the river now, it was climbing, apparently, to the very heart of the mountains. Tracy too had thought them far from civilisation, but she stared in delight at the small house that had just come into view.

It was a typical Slovenian house, with a wooden roof and low overhanging eaves. The car slowed as they passed and Tracy noticed a face turn to look out of the window. And then, looking past the house, she gasped.

A low, white sports car stood beside the house on a patch of grass. There was no-body in it, but a rucksack had been dropped on the ground beside it. Tracy stared as if mesmerised; and then she closed her eyes.

The white sports car was the one she had seen Melissa driving on the first day at Belanice. And the rucksack she had seen only yesterday, on the broad shoulders of Iain Macalister.

And, opening her eyes again, Tracy looked straight into the trees and caught a brief flash of colour; the dazzling electric blue of a kingfisher. The colour of Melissa's sweater and pants.

They had lunch at the mountain hut, right under the face of the Triglav. The hut was large – much too big to be called a hut, Tracy thought – and they were served by a smiling Slovenian who spoke no English but was able to converse fluently in German. They were given large bowls of steaming goulash, followed by fresh fruit – Tracy thought briefly of the journey bringing provisions to this out-of-the-way place –

and cream-topped *turske* coffee.

'And now I'm too full to move,' Mrs Marchant announced. 'I shall go and sit on one of those seats outside and stare at this enormous mountain. You can come with me, Jim, and leave these two to go exploring on their own for a while. They've been stuck with us long enough!'

'Mrs Marchant, you're an angel,' Nick declared. He followed them out to the terrace and settled the older woman comfortably in a chair. 'We'll be about an hour or so, I expect, if that's all right with you?'

'Fine. And don't go climbing that mountain!'

It would be easier to do that than to do what she had decided she must, Tracy thought in some confusion. Her heart beat rapidly as they walked side by side along the stony track, the mountain like a massive grey wall in front of them. But she could put it off no longer. It wasn't fair to Nick to let him go on like this – happy in the belief that she was in love with him, wanted to marry him. He was too nice to deceive; too nice to hurt as she was going to hurt him.

'Nick–' she began, but Nick, glancing quickly behind to see that they were out of sight of the hut, stopped and took her in his arms. Tracy stiffened, but his lips sought hers, intent, sweet; the kisses, she thought involuntarily, of a boy.

'Nick, I've got to talk to you.'

He released her, staring down at her troubled face. Then he turned and walked on, Tracy following miserably. Already, she thought, he was hurt; already the pain had begun. And, with the pain of an impossible love searing her own heart, she knew just what it was going to do to him.

'All right,' he said at last. 'Talk. I suppose I've known there was something wrong all along. I suppose that's why I wanted to kiss you – to stop you talking, to keep it all for just a little while longer. But you go ahead, Tracy – talk. Tell me what's on your mind.'

'Nick – we can't talk like this, walking. Please stop a minute.' She glanced around, gestured at a fallen tree. 'Let's sit down.'

'Okay.' He looked absurdly like a small boy, she thought, his mouth almost sulky, his eyes hidden by drooping lashes. 'Go on, Tracy. Get it over.'

'I think you know what I'm going to say.' She spoke slowly, aware that Nick was perhaps more observant than she had at first thought. 'Nick, I've been thinking – and I don't think I can marry you after all.' She

166

closed her eyes for a moment, swallowed and went on. 'You see, I – I don't know very much about love. I've never had any boy-friends, never been in love before. I don't really know – what it's all about. It would be wrong of me to – to promise to marry you and then let you down. Except that that's just what I *am* doing,' she added wryly.

There was a long pause.

'Well?' Nick said at last. 'Is that all?'

'All?'

'Yes, all. Isn't there any more you want to tell me? Like, you've met someone else. Like, there's someone at home you came away to forget and now you realise you love him after all. Like, oh, I don't know. But it can't be as simple as you make out.'

'Simple?' Tracy thought of the pain of indecision, her reluctance to abandon their plans – for even when she acknowledged her love for Iain, she had still considered the possibility of becoming Nick's wife. After all, Iain was out of her reach – life with Nick, even as second best, might be a great deal better than a lonely existence in her cottage in Herefordshire. And then she had known that even this was out of the question – that she could neither betray her love, unspoken and impossible though it might

167

ever be, nor give Nick a love that wasn't wholly sincere.

Nick was looking at her, his brown eyes puzzled, hurt – and angry.

'Yes, simple,' he said. 'A few days ago you agreed to marry me. Now you go back on it. There must be a reason. It can't just be that you don't know your own mind!'

'Oh yes it can!' Tracy cried, forgetting that she would once have refuted indignantly any suggestion that she "didn't know her own mind". 'I've told you – I haven't been around much, I don't have much experience. There *isn't* any other reason.' Nothing – nothing – would make her confess that it was her feelings for Iain Macalister that had changed her mind.

'Well, then that's all right.' Nick's face cleared. 'It's just nerves. Don't worry about it, Tracy. It's like you said – too much happening too quickly. You've just got a bit het-up.'

'No – it's not like that,' she began helplessly; but Nick was smiling again, his old cheerful self and she floundered to a stop. 'Well, perhaps – but Nick, I'm *not* sure. Please – will you release me from the engagement? Can't we just be friends for a little longer – till I *am* sure?' *And then, when we've got home and you can see things differently too – then we can drift apart. It won't hurt so much – and it won't spoil your holiday now.*

But she didn't voice these thoughts. Feeling guilty, because she knew in her heart that she ought not to let Nick go on thinking she might love him, she gazed at him – and saw his teeth flash in the familiar grin.

'It'll be all right, darling,' he told her comfortingly. 'You'll see. I expect I've rushed you too much. Just tell me this – there *isn't* anyone else is there? No young man waiting in Hereford?'

Wordlessly, Tracy shook her head.

'Then everything's all right. I won't rush you any more, Tracy. But when we get back to England – well, I shall want a proper answer then!' And he smiled at her, tipped her chin with his fingers and kissed her gently on the lips. 'Don't forget, now!'

The track led onward, climbing more steeply now. Tracy followed Nick, confused and uncertain. In some ways, what had happened was all for the best – Nick was still happy and she could – she supposed – consider herself free of the engagement. But she was painfully aware that she had, inadvertently given him quite the wrong impression. He was clearly convinced that her sudden change of heart was a mere attack of nerves – something she would recover from, to his advantage.

However, there was nothing she could do about it now. And it would be little short of a crime not to enjoy the beautiful countryside, imprint it on her mind, every detail observed. At the very least, Aunt Chloe would want a full description; and Tracy knew that she herself would regret it later if she allowed the remainder of the holiday to be spoiled by doubts.

As she pondered, the track opened up; the trees on either side gave way to a stretch of grass, like a pool of green under the shadowy mountain. Flop-eared Nubian goats grazed, their coats cream-coloured and woolly; a dairyman's hut stood alone on a hummock and grey rocks jutted through the turf.

And above them and all around soared the grey face of the Triglav, Yugoslavia's highest mountain, immense, forbidding, stark. Tracy and Nick stood together, necks craned, eyes searching the topmost peaks. The snow glittered with sunshine against a clear blue sky. And as they watched, the silence of the valley was broken by the low roar of an avalanche somewhere up in those soaring peaks – a long, sonorous swelling of noise, rising to a crescendo before it died away to the muttering rumble of distant thunder. And a puff of snow, pale as smoke, billowed slowly against the cerulean sky and as slowly settled again.

It was the implication of tremendous events of which they could know nothing, that shook Tracy to the core. All the bewilderment of the past months – her father's illness and death, her confusion over Iain, her guilt over Nick – welled up inside her. She turned her face into Nick's shoulder and wept. And he, saying nothing, held her tightly against him. But what he was thinking, Tracy had no idea.

The walk back to the hut and the drive back to Belanice were quiet. Mrs Marchant, who was not strong, fell asleep soon after they reached the smooth main road. Mr Marchant concentrated on his driving and Nick and Tracy sat in the back. Tracy's hand lay on her knee and, after a moment's hesitation, Nick had taken it in his own, clasping it warmly. She did not withdraw it; the feeling of it there was comforting somehow, and Tracy was aware that just at present she was in desperate need of some human contact, just as under the mountain she had needed someone to hold her as she wept out all her confusion.

The day had been a strange one, and she wondered how all this emotion would appear once she was back in England, in the calmer countryside of Herefordshire. How much did landscape affect one? Once away from the wild, rugged mountains, would her emotions too become calmer, less tumultuous? Or would she have to live all her days with the memory of a brief passion awakened in an Alpine meadow under soaring grey peaks?

Her thoughts occupied her silently nearly all the way back to Belanice. But she found time, nevertheless to look out for a small cottage on the way down the rough, stony track; to notice whether a white sports car still stood on a patch of grass, whether a brown rucksack lay beside it or a girl in kingfisher pants walked in the woods.

There was nothing. The grass was bare, the cottage shuttered. And Tracy, her throat suddenly and inexplicably aching, turned her head away. Whether Iain Macalister and Melissa had been there that day, she would probably never know; just as she would probably never know why they should visit such a place; why they should visit an old woman in the village; or why Iain, who had never been to Yugoslavia in his life, should speak the language so fluently.

NINE

'Dear Aunt Chloe,' wrote Tracy, keeping her writing small in order to squeeze as much information as possible on the back of the postcard. 'Having a lovely time. Weather good. Scenery beautiful–' she paused, chewing her pen. What else was there to say – *I have fallen in love with one man who hates me, and got engaged to another man I don't love?* Aunt Chloe would think she had gone mad. And perhaps she had. Perhaps it was all really due to a reaction – reaction against the restricted form of her life for so long, the sudden access of freedom…

Tracy bit her lip at the implied criticism of her father. Telling herself that she was thinking nonsense again – that she would be well advised to forget all thoughts of romance and love, concentrating entirely on getting to know the country, she finished her post-card hastily with 'Tell you all about it later, love, Tracy.' And stood up.

She and Nick had agreed that they would continue to spend their time together– 'just because it's fun, if you want it that way,' he said, brown eyes on her face, 'but because we need to get to know each other as well.' And Tracy, who felt that if she didn't want Nick as a lover, she might well need him as a friend, had agreed thankfully.

Today they were going to make the long-promised trip to the top of the mountain by cable-car. The ski hotel itself was not open, but Nick's receptionist friend, Marela had told him that they could get lunch in one of the chalets. What this meant, Tracy had no idea, but she was content to wait to find out.

They had decided to walk along a wood-land path along the side of the mountain, not far above the road, which led to the cable-car terminus. Tracy pulled on her walking boots, thankful once more that she had brought them. Glancing out of the window, she noticed that the sky was slightly overcast, the lake a metallic grey instead of its usual blue. She pushed an extra pullover into her scarlet rucksack and slipped her arms into an anorak.

'You're all dressed up for mountaineering, I see,' Nick greeted her a few minutes later. 'I suppose you're wise though – if there's snow on top, it's probably cold. Hang on a minute, I'll get another sweater.'

Tracy waited in the airy hall, admiring the pot-plants and the decorative floor tiles. The Yugoslavians did these rather well, she thought; it would be nice to take a few home. But they were probably very heavy and she was aware that her luggage had been too near the weight limit when coming to be able to take much back. Aunt Chloe would have to be content with very light souvenirs of Tracy's enforced holiday!

Nick rejoined her, resplendent in a thick Scandinavian sweater, and they swung cheerfully away down the hill, nodding good-morning to the Marchants as they went. Melissa's white sports car passed them, with Melissa alone at the wheel, and they waved to her, Nick rather more enthusiastically than Tracy.

'Wonder where the Macalister is?' he mused. 'Not usually far from Melissa's side, is he? I suppose she has to work, though – she goes to the offices in Bled and Ljubljana quite a lot, I believe. And the Macalister has

175

to amuse himself.'

Which he did to some effect, Tracy thought, recalling with a warm shame the day she had spent with him, and its outcome. For a while, they had been in accord, and the knowledge had been a joy as heady as wine. But he had, it seemed, merely been "amusing himself" – and then had had the audacity to call *her* a butterfly!

'What d'you reckon?' Nick asked, and she realised that he had asked her a question.

'Oh, sorry – I was wandering again. What was it you said?'

'You know,' Nick said gently. 'If we are to be married ever – not that I'm suggesting such a thing, you understand, the subject being taboo – but if we were, I might begin to find this habit of yours somewhat irritating.'

Tracy turned and stared at him, her eyes wide with surprise. 'Habit? What habit? Nick, what *are* you talking about?'

'It doesn't matter.' He was laughing. 'I just asked you if you agreed with me that the travel agents are going to have to find themselves a new courier before very long.'

'A new courier?' Tracy was bewildered. 'I just don't know what–'

'My dear dimwit – Melissa and Iain. Don't

you think they're rather friendly? Wedding bells – or don't you see it?'

'Oh!' For a moment, she was nonplussed. Then she realised that Nick had only put into words what she had herself suspected, and the hot betraying colour ran up into her cheeks. She turned away from Nick's curious stare and said quickly, 'Oh, I don't know – perhaps. But they – they don't – I mean, I haven't seen–'

'No, they don't make it obvious, I agree. It's just that they do seem to be on very friendly terms.' He was watching her thoughtfully. 'However, it's none of our business, is it? And not really interesting, either. And here's our path through the woods. Shall I go first, to fend off bears and wolves?'

'You don't suppose there're any around here, do you?' Tracy was glad of a chance to change the subject.

'No, not down here near the road. Not at ten in the morning, anyway! But I suppose there might be some further up in the mountains. Better be careful coming down!'

'Oh, Nick you're not still thinking of walking down, are you? I'm sure it's not safe. There's still snow up there.'

'Mm, not much though. It's only a cover-

177

ing now, Tracy. Anyway, we won't try it unless we think it's safe.' He stopped suddenly, blocking Tracy's view of the path ahead. 'Hey, look at this! A young glacier!'

Tracy peered past him. They had arrived at a narrow gully, where evidently a stream had carved a channel down the side of the mountain. It was filled now, however, not with water but with snow – hard-packed frozen snow, solid as ice, sprawling down the gully like the overflow from a giant ice-cream cornet.

'Well, if that's a sample of what's at the top, I don't want to know,' Tracy said firmly. 'Can we cross it?'

'Oh, yes, I think so. It's firm enough.' Nick stepped gingerly across it, testing each step with an outstretched foot. 'Come on – just mind you don't slide, it's slippery in places. Take you all the way down to the road, that would, and you'd have all that climbing to do again!'

Tracy stepped cautiously across, flinging herself at Nick and giggling as she reached the other side. For a moment he held her; then, letting her go rather suddenly, he said with a curious edge in his voice: 'Well, no good hanging about here – we've still got quite a way to go.'

They walked on in silence for a while. Tracy felt oddly hurt, though she knew she had no right to. It was Nick who was hurt – and if it made him bitter too, she must take the blame. She hoped it wouldn't though, and felt again that she had been incredibly childish and blind to have let things get this far.

It took them an hour to walk along the path to the terminus, and they crossed several more of Nick's 'young glaciers' on the way. Tracy enjoyed them – they gave her a sense of adventure and she wondered if, after all, they might be able to walk down the mountain. It might be fun to try.

Going up in the cable-car, she was not so sure. Seen as close as this, with the car crawling up the steep crags, sandwiched in a deep crevice in the rock face, the cruelty of the mountain seemed to grip her soul. There would be no quarter given here, no mercy on those who trifled with such implacable territory. The landscape seemed alien, hostile. Tracy felt again that beside these immensities, the human lot was so frail, so puny as to be totally insignificant.

She scrambled out of the cable-car at the top, shivering in the sudden cold, and stood gazing about her.

'It's like being on the Moon,' she said slowly. 'I never thought a mountain-top would be like this... All those hummocks, the little paths. All the chalets. It's like a village – a village on the Moon.'

A few fir-trees were grouped here and there in the snow, which lay deep in the hollows. Apart from those and the wooden chalets that were dotted about, mostly on the tops of hummocks and knolls, the landscape was empty. There were no peaks, no rocky points; just a frozen waste, stretching beyond the vision.

'I don't think I like it much,' Tracy said suddenly, feeling again the unfriendliness of the atmosphere on this mountain.

'Come round the other side of the hotel,' Nick suggested. 'We should be able to see down into the valley.'

They stood on a wide balcony, their hair lifted by the breeze, and gazed down. Nick was right; the entire valley lay spread beneath them, the lake dark and mysterious, the village like toys. The trees that skirted the lower slopes of the hills were like blades of grass, or cushions of moss. Tracy remembered that they were over five thousand feet high – higher than any mountain in Britain. She stared down, fascinated by the extreme 'smallness' of everything.

'One of those chalets is going to serve us lunch,' Nick remarked. 'Shall we go and find it?'

The top of the mountain seemed to be networked with paths, many of them – to Tracy's amusement – signposted. The sense of being in a village, somehow cut off from the outside world grew stronger; but when they peered into the windows of some of the chalets they found them obviously un-occupied.

'Ski-ing's over, I suppose,' Nick said. 'These are like weekend cottages, aren't they. It must be a real little community in winter. Look, there are even lamp-posts on the paths!'

'Lamp-posts on a mountain top!' The whole thing seemed too bizarre for words. Tracy was still giggling when they found the chalet that still served meals, by arrange-ment with their hotel.

She was, however amused, delighted with the chalet. It was slightly larger than most of the others and had a large balcony, with the best view of the lake and mountains oppo-site that Tracy had seen so far. Inside, it was warm and cosy; the walls were thick, and clad with wood; the windows, of course, double-glazed, and into the centre of the room jutted a great tiled stove that in winter would be kept stoked full, becoming an enormous radiator to keep cold at bay.

Their hostess was a buxom Slovenian, swarthy and smiling, her mouth displaying a fine set of golden teeth. She chattered volubly in German, showing them to a table beside the window, and disappeared into the kitchen.

Tracy and Nick sat silent. She wondered what he was thinking about. His brown eyes, usually so open and merry, were remote, fixed on the far peaks of the mountain. His hands, which Tracy had grown quite accustomed to holding, now cupped his chin as he gazed broodingly out of the window. For the first time, Tracy realised that she had done him more than an injustice. In thinking of him as a boy, fun to be with, she had belittled his own capacity for emotion. He was not a boy; he was a man. It was the boy in him who had first attracted her with his sense of fun; his enjoyment of life; it was the man who had fallen in love, and it was the man she had hurt.

The Slovenian woman reappeared with a tray and set two steaming bowls of soup in front of them. Like the meal in the other mountain hut – was it really only yesterday? – the soup was more like goulash, full of meat and vegetables. It was especially welcome on top of this strange mountain, and Tracy and Nick ate it with gusto.

They were about half-way through when footsteps announced the arrival of another guest; and turning round, Tracy beheld – as she might have guessed she would – the shuttered, stony face of Iain Macalister.

He glanced at her briefly, nodded, and spoke to Nick. 'Good lunch?'

'Very good. Goulash. Or whatever they call it. Join us?'

The Scot hesitated, glanced at Tracy and made up his mind. 'If you don't mind.'

He sat down. The two men eyed each other, almost like two dogs wondering whether or not to fight. Tracy felt the tension in the air, the electric quality of the silence. She glanced from one to the other.

'Come up in the cable-car?' Nick inquired, and the Scotsman's eyebrows shot up.

'Is there another way?'

'The path. We were thinking of going down that way.' Nick took a mouthful of goulash.

'If you'll take my advice, you'll forget that idea. The path's not safe.'

Tracy saw Nick's mouth tighten and knew a moment of sympathy; really, the hateful Scot was too arrogant and conceited for words. But she had an uncomfortable feeling that in this he might be right.

'Well, I'll have a look at it first.' Nick's tone was easy, but Tracy recognised the obstinacy in the words. He was not going to be ordered about by Iain Macalister! And neither, she decided at once, was she.

'I think that would be a good idea,' she said and was immediately aware of Iain's gaze on her.

'You're surely not thinking of attempting this too? You must be crazy!'

'Oh, must I? And what business is it of yours?' She stopped as the woman returned with Iain's goulash. She took away their empty bowls and returned, gold smile flashing, with two plates of pancakes folded into triangles. Tracy began to eat, seething.

'It's my business if you get lost, or killed!'

'Is it? And what makes you think I will be, anyway?'

There was a short silence. Tracy glanced up and got the impression that Iain was fighting for control. When he spoke at last, it was a strange, tight voice.

'Please – take notice of me. The path isn't safe. You'd be foolish – mad, yes, mad – to try it. It's not worth it. Don't ever speak to me again, if you like – but don't try walking down that path!'

He was gazing at Tracy as he said it, his eyes dark and intense. For a moment, her heart twisted painfully. It was the first time she had seen him since she realised she loved him. Yet he still had the power to fire her with rage, to blind her to reason. She finished her pancake and sipped at coffee which appeared – as if by magic – at her elbow.

'Thank you for your advice, Mr Macalister,' she said politely. 'We'll bear it in mind.' And she turned deliberately from him and gazed out of the window.

They left the chalet while Iain was still drinking his coffee, and walked down the path. Tracy was feeling a little calmer now. She was aware that Iain was probably right in saying that the path was unsafe – after all, Melissa had said so, and she hadn't been too keen on it herself. But she agreed with Nick that it would do no harm to look, and together they followed the signpost which pointed the way down.

'Well, it's clear so far,' Nick remarked. 'Clearer than the other side. No snow at all here. We should be able to cross that bit down there, and once we get past the snow line we'll have no trouble. These paths are obviously pretty regularly used.'

'Mmm… Nick?'

'What?'

'We will turn back, won't we – if it does get tricky further down?'

'Of course we will. You can trust me.' He grinned at her, but there was an edge to his voice, a tightness in his smile that she had not noticed before. She remembered the curious look he had given her that morning when they had discussed Iain and Melissa; his wary hostility towards Iain just now…

'Don't do it just to spite Iain,' she heard herself saying, and was startled by his re-action. He turned and stared at her, his face and voice like a stranger's.

'You're talking nonsense. I thought it was *you* who hated him – not me. Now – are you coming, or aren't you?' And he wheeled away, striding down the path, his back rigid.

Tracy followed him. It was true that the path seemed clear – although further down, where it disappeared into the firs, she could see a good deal of snow. And when they reached it Nick, stepping carefully, found his leg sinking in well beyond the knee.

'We'd better go round the edge. Keep to the trees, there's not so much snow under them where it's hummocky. I don't suppose it goes far – we can work round it all right.'

Doubtfully, Tracy followed him, keeping above the deeper parts of the snow. She wanted to suggest going back, but sensed that Nick was trying desperately to salvage a rather drastic loss of confidence – and, since she was the cause of that loss, felt bound to do all she could to help him.

Slowly, they worked their way along the edge of the snow. It was difficult to see where the path went; presumably it followed the line of the small valley it had entered, but after a while Tracy began uneasily to wonder if it were indeed still there. Surely they had crossed at least one small ridge? The valleys – little more than gullies running down the side of the mountain – all looked alike. It would be only too easy, on taking your eyes off the way for a moment, to turn slightly and walk in quite the wrong direction.

Tracy turned to look back, hoping for the comforting sight of the mountain top, with its chalets, its zig-zagging paths and its incongruous lamp-posts.

She saw nothing; nothing but the mountain, white with snow, its deathly colour spattered with the darkness of jutting rocks and tall fir trees. Beyond that she saw grey, lowering clouds. There was nothing else.

Already they had come further down the mountain than she had supposed. Already, they must have turned – not once, but many times – losing the path as they worked along under the trees.

It might be possible to go back; but Nick was far ahead now, scrambling down the edge of a long, steep slope of snow. She opened her mouth to call, then remembered the avalanche they had seen and heard yesterday – wasn't it true that a shout could start one off? And once down that slope, she doubted whether Nick would be able to climb up it again. It would be infinitely worse if they were to be separated.

Slowly, and with the beginnings of panic in her heart, Tracy began to crawl down the slope towards him.

Nick had realised she was behind and stopped to wait.

'Quite an adventure, this, isn't it?' he grinned, a trifle uneasily, Tracy thought.

'Still, we should be below the snow-line soon – it'll be easy then.'

'If we can find the path.'

'Well, of course we will – we can't be far from it now. Look, don't start getting all panicky, Tracy – it won't help. It's all right, I tell you. Macalister's an old woman.'

Tracy said nothing. She gazed around them – down the steep slope where snow, untrodden and white, disappeared into fir trees that seemed to stretch on for ever. She turned and stared up at the slopes above, the cruel jagged rocks to the right, the rounded hummocks, thick with trees to the left; the deep, snowfilled valleys in between.

They had left too few footprints in their careful working round the trees, to be able to go back. And she was convinced that they had strayed far from the path.

'After all,' Nick said, 'We've only got to go *down*. We're bound to find the path again – and there must be more than one anyway.'

He was worried too, she thought detachedly. And pictured the side of the mountain – a grey mass of jagged rocks, sheer cliffs, high unclimbable precipices. You might scramble about them for ever and never find the path; end on top of a great cliff, with a thousand foot drop at your feet; lose your footing and slip, bouncing like a tossed pebble on the treacherous slope…

She became aware of Nick's eyes on her face, and shook herself. It would do no good to think of things like that. Nick was right when he said panic wouldn't help. And she could scarcely blame him … she had been as keen as he to prove Iain wrong – at first.

The thought of Iain came to her mind like a keen wind, blowing away the last traces of bitterness. She knew that, although he might not love her, although he might be marrying Melissa, although she might never see him again after this holiday, yet she owed it to him at least to acknowledge that he had been right. She owed it to him to forget their sparring – and what had it all been about, after all? Some spilt coffee, a few heated words, squabbles in which she had been as much to blame as he. Behaviour that seemed now to be quite incredibly childish.

If for no other reason, she had to get down this mountain in order to put things right with Iain. She stared down the long, never-ending slope, the snow which stretched much further than they had thought, the dark fir trees which lay like a shadow across the depths.

'Nick—' she was suddenly frightened, '—wouldn't it be better to try to go back? I – I don't like this at all. I'm not even sure we're going in the right direction.'

He spoke impatiently. 'Of course we are. Look, I told you, Tracy – panic won't help. What's the matter with you? And we can't go back – you must see that. We've come too far now to think of it.'

They stared at each other and Tracy, realising for the first time just how young and immature were the lines of his face, acknowledged that in this he was right. There was no going back. Whatever lay before them, must be faced and – she prayed – overcome.

'It's perfectly all right,' Nick said more gently. 'The snow can't go much further.'

'All right. We can't go back. So let's go on. As you said, there *is* only one way – down.'

And her words were almost lost in a sudden roar of noise, a tremendous crack as if the mountain itself was splitting, and Tracy looked up in sudden terror, almost expecting to see the very rock itself come tumbling about their heads. There must, she realised an instant later, have been a flash, unnoticed by them; and even as she thought this there was a second, a sudden brilliant splitting of the clouds and immediately a loud crack, as if someone had fired a rifle in her ear. The thunder rolled menacingly on the mountain; the lowering clouds let fall a sudden splatter of rain; and Tracy found that she was holding Nick's hand tightly.

'Well, that's all we needed!' His cheerfulness was more than strained as he searched her eyes. 'You're not scared of thunder, are you, Tracy?'

She managed to summon up a smile as she shook her head. 'Not in normal circumstances! But on an unknown mountain in a foreign country – and amongst all these great trees – I can't say I like it much!'

'Well, there's no point in trying to shelter. We'll just have to press on.' He squeezed her hands and let them go. 'Keep to the edge of the snow, darling. We'll be all right, I promise you.'

The task of keeping one's feet on the steep, slippery slopes of a snow-clad mountain was sufficient, Tracy found, to make quite unimportant the mere fact that thunder and lightning were rending the air, that hail was stinging one's face, and rain rapidly soaking through too thin waterproofs. She was aware of the discomforts, but they seemed minor in comparison to the gigantic problem of finding the path and getting safely back to the road. The flashing and crashing overhead was a kind of background music. It was frightening if you let yourself think about it – terrifying in its grandeur, this battle of the elements. The whole of life seemed to be reduced to a question of weather – a weather whose immensity she had never guessed at, never imagined. Now, pausing as Nick felt in a patch of snow for the safest part, Tracy watched the lightning glow briefly on the trees, invest the snow with a strange, eerie glimmer. She listened to the violence of the thunder, thought of snow falling on the bare slopes, constant, inexorable, covering everything with its thick white blanket. If you were lost here when it began to fall, it would take months before your body was found … if it was ever found… And then she saw a long, thin blade of lightning reach down from the sky, saw it touch a tree and the tree blaze into sudden flames as it toppled. The crack was instantaneous, the sound of the tree falling combined with the bellow of thunder.

Iain. She must think of Iain. She had to see him again, to tell him…

Tell him what? What must she tell him?

Tracy did not know, she could not think; she knew only that she had something important to tell him, something he must know, something that could not wait.

She had to get down this mountain, to see Iain again.

TEN

There were Christmas roses growing at the edge of the snow, their petals pale, green and mauve. They seemed to bloom as soon as the snow had melted. Christmas roses, blooming where the snows had been...

Surely, now they must be close to the edge of the snowline.

It seemed that for the whole of her life, she had been doing this, scrambling down a mountain that had no end. Bent double, hands clutching at rocks, ever-mindful of the terrible drop that lay below; ringed round by unfriendly grey peaks, ruthless against a grey sky. Trees below, their rounded, leafy tops looking like moss under a microscope. The valley floor still out of sight. Nick ahead, seldom looking back, intent on keeping his feet... Thunder in her ears; eyes dazed by lightning...

Once, she caught a glimpse of the valley, far below; a toy village clustered around the end of a pewter-coloured lake. Houses, almost too small to recognise; a tiny dot that might have been a car or a lorry. Then it was hidden again by the trees, thousands of trees. And Tracy was glad. The realisation of just how far it yet was to the bottom, had made her feel sick.

They had come below the snow-line at last, and Nick waited for her. He was pale, his brown eyes no longer merry. But he had a smile for her, and his hands were firm on her arms.

'We've made it, Tracy!'

'Made it?' Her voice was dull. It had stopped raining, she noticed vaguely. The woods were silent. The slope fell away below them, brown earth disappearing in the darkness below the trees.

'We'll find the path now, all right, you'll see.' He grinned at her, but it was a forced imitation of his usual ready grin. 'Not still scared, are you, Tracy?'

She withdrew herself from his arms and said, 'Let's get down, Nick. It's gone four.'

'Oh, it won't be long now. It was supposed to take two and a half hours on the path – we'll only be another hour or so now.'

'We've taken two hours already.'

'Yes – so it can't be long now. Look, Tracy, we'll go to the right I think – by my reckoning, we should pick up the path fairly soon. Then all we have to do is follow it!'

It sounded easy, but to Tracy, staring at the steep, treacherous slope, it looked impossible. The earth, recently released from snow, was loose and unstable. It became a matter of groping from tree to tree, afraid to let go of one before grasping the next. A matter of testing every foothold before you trusted your weight to it, crawling across the face of the mountain, hands scrabbling for something to cling to. It was hard, aching work, and impossibly, painfully slow.

And then Nick, ahead, gave a cry of triumph and Tracy scrambled to catch him up.

'The path!' He pointed exultantly to a narrow trail that led away between the trees. It looked scarcely wider than a sheep track – but undoubtedly someone – or something – had come this way. And it was infinitely

196

better than crawling across a loose moun-ain-face, with no more support than the roots of the trees.

'Oh, Nick!' For a moment, Tracy felt weak. But she couldn't afford to relax yet; there was still a long, long way to go. 'But which way? We don't want to find ourselves going up again!'

'Well, if we do we just turn and come down again!' Nick's spirits were rising almost visibly. 'Anyway, we should be able to get along a bit faster now. All right?'

They set off along the track. It was cer-tainly easier going than the treacherous snow or the trackless mountain face, but was still exceptionally rough. Tracy could not remember ever having crossed such dif-ficult country; even on the last few walks she had done with her father in the Lake District before his final illness began, she could not recall slopes as steep as this, ground as treacherous. And certainly there had been nothing as high.

It was perhaps the height that scared her so much; the knowledge that even now, after nearly three hours, they might still be close to the top of the mountain... Seen from below, there had seemed to be little snow except on the highest peaks. Their progress had been so slow they still had the major part of the descent to make.

She thought again of Iain. She would see him again; tell him what had seemed so important; and then they would say goodbye. Her heart contracted painfully at the thought of saying goodbye, or watching the strong, proud Scot walk away from her for a life she could never share. She looked at Nick, feeling his way carefully over a rough part of the path ahead, contemplated his young body, his boyish bearing, and wondered how she ever could have looked on him as a possible husband. He was still a boy – feckless, irresponsible. Meaning no harm, he had risked their lives through his own obstinacy, his own lack of forethought and refusal to take advice. No – she could never share her life with Nick Lester. A sense of fun, a pair of merry brown eyes were not enough; they did not add up to love.

The faint, narrow path turned down and passed a rocky outcrop. For a moment, Nick disappeared from Tracy's view; she had a sudden hollow feeling that she was alone on the unfriendly mountain, and then she heard his voice.

'Tracy! Look at this!'

'What?' It was impossible to hurry. Cling-ing to the rough face of the rock, she edged round it.

Nick was standing a little below her, his face upturned and glowing. He was on a broad, grassy path; a path such as one might have found in any English wood; a path leading firmly along the side of the moun-tain.

'Oh, thank goodness!' Tracy scrambled down to join him, stood at his side. She wriggled her rucksack from her shoulders. 'Let's celebrate.'

'Chocolate!' Nick said admiringly. 'Well, you *are* clever, Tracy – fancy keeping it this long. But we'd better only have a small bit now.' He accepted a square and grinned at her. 'It's still a long time to dinner!'

Side by side, they swung along the path. Tracy felt light with relief, almost weak after the slow painful process across the side of the mountain. She glanced down, caught a glimpse of trees far below. Nick was right – there was still a long way to go. But it was all right now – now that they were on the path.

And then, turning a bend, they stopped. Tracy's heart sank, her limbs heavy; tears threatened her eyes. The path – still broad, still grassy – was partly blocked by fallen trees. And beyond that, they could see the wide, grey slope of a snow-filled gully. At the other side, the path disappeared into a dark, gaping hole in the rocks.

'What is it?' she whispered, thoughts of wolves and bears in her mind.

'I don't know.' He spoke slowly. 'And I don't think we can get across there. That snow is ready to give way at any moment. This may be a path, but I don't think it's ours. Perhaps it's an old mine working, or something like that – perhaps a hideout.' He glanced at the slope of the snow in the gully. 'I wonder if we can work our way down beside that.'

'Oh, no, Nick – please!' But he was already scrambling over the fallen trees, feeling his way down the slope to find the best way across, pushing his way through the tumbled branches.

Tracy followed him. The thought of climbing down beside the gully terrified her, but there was nothing else to do. She was desperately aware that, whatever else happened, they must not get separated.

Oh, Iain, she thought sadly, clinging to a young tree as Nick slithered and scrambled towards the gully. Iain, Iain – shall I ever see you again?

'You can't climb down there, it's too dangerous,' she called. And then, as Nick took no notice, '*I* can't climb down there – I won't even try – it's not *possible*, Nick!' She could see him peering down the gully. What could he see? Did it stretch away before him, for thousands of feet, losing itself in the forests that clothed the lowest slopes? Was he seriously thinking of going down it? Tracy closed her eyes. One false step – one slithering stone under your foot – and there would be nothing to stop you in a wild, hurtling rush to the bottom.

A sudden anger filled her; anger that he should have brought her here, exposed her to such risks.

'Nick, I'm going back! I'm going back to the path, back the way we came, and if we haven't got down by the time it's dark–' she glanced at her watch and her heart lurched; only two hours daylight left! 'I'm going to stop where I am and not move!' She turned and began to climb back to the path.

'Wait for me – Tracy, wait!' He was scrambling back towards her, crawling on hands and knees up the slope, pulling himself up by tree-roots and branches. 'You're right, we couldn't possibly climb down there.' He stood beside her, breathless. 'All right, we'll get on to the path and go the other way. There must be a way down!'

But the path seemed to have disappeared from the mountain. Perhaps they had climbed further down than they had realised; perhaps the steepness of the slopes had deceived them; perhaps they had lost their bearings completely. Whatever the reason, that broad, grassy track had vanished as completely as if it had never been. They were back to scrambling, crawling along the mountain-side, hardly caring now whether they went up or down, aware only that they must go on – go on for as long as possible, for only by going on was there any hope at all of ever finding a way down.

They did not speak. Tracy's mind was too full. She thought of Aunt Chloe, arranging this holiday in the hope that it might take her mind off her recent tragedy, help her to make a new life. New life! Well, perhaps it had – but for how long? How long could you survive on a cold, hostile mountain? A night – a day? And what of wolves, bears – what occupied that cave they had seen, what used that broad grassy track?

She thought of Iain, who had known the danger they faced, had warned them –

begged them – not to go. Iain, whom she loved, had always loved without even realising it. She remembered their complete accord at Lipice, and again beside the gorge and in the green, bowl-like valley. Her lips burned at the memory of his kisses and she closed her eyes in sudden pain. Was that all the love she was ever to know? Was she to die on this mountain, lost and wandering, and never, never to see Iain again?

At that moment, she hated Nick. And when at last they stood together on a rocky promontory, the sheer cliffs falling away below them, the steep valley ringed by sheer, jagged rocks, she sank down on to a tuft of heather and buried her head in her arms.

'Tracy.' His voice was gentle, his hands trembled slightly on her shoulders. 'Tracy, don't be so frightened. We'll get down all right, I promise you.'

'How can you promise that?' she blazed at him, raising her head suddenly. 'How *can* you? You've never been here before – you don't know what lies below us? How are we to cross this valley – look at the cliffs. You may be a climber, Nick, but I'm not – I can't cope with it. And we haven't got ropes or anything, none of the right equipment.' She let her head fall again, feeling tears trickle slowly between her fingers. 'We're never going to get down, never find our way back.'

'There must be a way,' he said, but his voice was unconvinced. 'Tracy, we must keep on trying. There's – there's nothing else to do.' And then, sharply. 'Don't cry, Tracy – please don't.' He lifted her hands away from her face and they stared into each other's eyes. A new humility was in his face and voice as he said quietly. 'I was wrong. I'm sorry I came, and I'm even sorrier that I brought you. But we're here now – and we have to go on trying.' He hesitated, and went on, 'I just want you to know – I think now is a time to be honest – I do love you. Very, very much. And I know that you don't love me. There *is* someone else, isn't there?'

Tracy looked away, down into the deep, narrow valley. She saw the gullies of frozen snow, imagined them suddenly giving way – as soon they must, the melted snow rushing headlong into the lake at the very bottom. The unfriendly rocks stared back at her, implacable, unyielding. And she knew that Nick was right; in conditions like these there was no room for anything short of complete honesty.

'Yes, Nick there is,' she answered steadily. 'I'm sorry. I didn't realise it myself at first.'

'Macalister?' he asked, and she nodded.

'I think I've known it for some time,' he said. 'The way he looks at you – the way–'

'Oh, he doesn't love me! He doesn't even know! I just – I shall have to forget him. But I couldn't marry you, Nick – feeling like that.'

He said nothing for a moment, then nodded, a queer finality in his face. 'No, I see that. So we'll be – just good friends.' A bitter smile twisted his mouth. 'Anyway, Tracy, we can't sit here discussing it. Let's have another bit of that chocolate – and then we'll try again.'

But it was only a few minutes later, as they edged cautiously along the narrow ledge that ran along the top of the precipice, that the accident happened.

Nick was just out of sight. He had found what seemed to be another path – faint, almost invisible at times, but still reappearing, taking them over rocks, under boulders, across loose scree. Nick, a short way ahead, had disappeared under a wide overhang, clinging to the face of the cliff as he edged along – and then Tracy heard a sharp exclamation, the sliding of loose stones, a cry.

A shower of earth, pebbles and rocks came into view, bouncing down the mountainside in great leaps, disappearing into the darkness of the woods. And then there was silence.

Her heart in her mouth, she edged as fast as she dared to the bend where Nick had disappeared.

He was still there. He was sitting against a tree-root, wedged between it and the rock-face. His leg was stuck out in front of him, and his face was white and twisted with pain.

'Oh, Nick – what have you done?'

'It's my ankle – I've done something to it. Sprained it – broken it – I don't know. I – don't think I can walk, Tracy.'

She stared at him. He looked very small, huddled there. Like a little boy; pale, scared and unhappy. His air of leadership, of cheerful assumption that everything would be all right, if only because he was Nick Lester, had fallen away from him. What was left looked helpless, vulnerable and very frightened.

'So what do we do now?' Tracy said slowly. 'I can't go on alone. I can't leave you here. And yet – if we just stay here, there's no hope at all.'

'You'll have to get help.'

'But I can't! I don't know the way down – or even if there *is* a way down! I might fall myself, break a leg or something. Or I might not be able to find the way back. You – you'd just lie here, alone, and never be found. Neither of us would ever be found.'

'We really are in a jam, aren't we?' Nick said after a minute.

'Yes. And it's getting dark.' Tracy looked at her watch. 'It's gone seven – nearly half past. It will be completely dark in half an hour. I can't go, Nick, I'd never get down in that time and I daren't move once it's dark.'

It was very quiet. The rain had stopped long ago and no wind stirred the trees. A cuckoo called somewhere; and then something else.

'What was that? It sounded like a voice!'

'It couldn't have been – who else–' Tracy began, but Nick raised a hand to silence her.

'It is, I tell you. Shout, Tracy. Shout anything!'

Together, half-doubtingly, they shouted. Shouted again and again, until Tracy's voice was hoarse and weak from shouting. And then they paused; and in the silence heard the shrill of a whistle.

'Iain! It must be Iain! He knew we were

coming – he's searching for us!' And Tracy raised her voice again, calling to Iain, calling to the man she loved to come to her, to rescue her from this terrible mountain, this awful, bottomless cliff. She called and called, hardly aware now of Nick who sat white and silent beside her, her thoughts and heart filled only with an urgent need, a desperate longing to see Iain again, to feel his hard body against hers, his strong arms holding her safe. And as she called, she heard the whistling come closer ... closer to the precipice where they huddled, closer, closer... And then she looked up, and he stood above her, his dark face scowling and smiling all at once, his expression full of something she dared not recognise in case it might not be true... And she scrambled to her feet and reached up to him, taking his hand, scrabbling to get up to him where he stood, unbelievably, on a path...

And then they were in each other's arms. Tracy clinging to him, half-laughing, tears on her cheeks. His head bent to hers, his voice hoarse as it muttered words she scarcely heard before their lips met in a long kiss; a kiss that searched out the emotions of their innermost hearts and told each of them all that they longed to know.

'Tracy!' he whispered at last, his voice husky. 'I thought you'd gone – I thought I'd lost you for ever.'

'Oh, Iain – Iain!' And they kissed again, murmuring incoherent endearments, lost to time in their joyful discovery of each other.

'I don't like to interrupt,' came a plaintive voice from below, 'But you haven't forgotten about me, have you?'

Iain looked startled, and Tracy laughed shakily. 'It's Nick – we were on the ledge below. We'd no idea there was a path here!'

'No – it's all too easy to be only a few feet from it and never know it's there.' He spoke gravely. 'Is Lester hurt? Are *you* all right, Tracy?'

'Yes – I'm fine, but Nick's done something to his ankle. He can't walk. We – we didn't know what to do.'

'Stay here.' Carefully, Iain swung himself down to the ledge and Tracy could hear him talking to Nick, examining the ankle. She listened anxiously, aware that their troubles were not yet over. They were on a path – but was it the right one? Had Iain come up from the road, or followed them down from the summit? And how were they to get Nick down the treacherous mountain, with an injured ankle?

Iain was back beside her, his face grim. 'We can't get him far tonight. It's almost dark – I daren't risk trying to move him until daylight. We'll have to get him to shelter, though.'

'You mean – we've got to stay here all night?'

He nodded. 'I'm afraid so. It's just not safe to do anything else. But don't worry, Tracy – I passed a hut a short way along the path. If we can only get him there, it will give shelter for the night. And it's light very early, don't forget that. We'll be all right.'

'Nick said that,' Tracy said slowly. 'That we will be all right. And I believed him at first. Then I didn't any more.'

'Do you believe me, Tracy?' Iain said, his eyes dark as he watched her, and she nodded.

'Yes, Iain, I believe you.'

'Then that's all that matters. Now–' he became brisk. 'We've got to get Nick up on to this path. It won't be very easy. Can you help?'

'What do you want me to do?'

'I think, if you stay here and I go down again... Be ready to help him up. I'll support him from below. Remember, he can't put any weight on his right foot. You'll have to try to take all his weight for a moment.' He paused, his eyes on her slim body. 'Do you think you'll be able to manage?'

'Oh, yes,' Tracy answered, remembering the times she had had to support her father when he became too weak to do things for himself. 'I'm quite used to that sort of thing.'

Iain glanced at her oddly, but made no comment. He swung himself over the edge again and she heard him talking to Nick, telling him what they were going to do. Then there was the sound of movement; a grunting from both men as they struggled to get Nick on to his feet. Nick's head appeared just below her, with Iain beside him. Slowly, grasping at the young trees which grew everywhere, Nick began to crawl up to the path.

Tracy stretched a hand down to him. She lay on the path, reaching down, praying that none of them would slip, for there would be little to save any of them. She felt for Nick's hand in hers, supported it strongly, felt him nearer, his weight dragging on her arm... And then he was beside her on the path, his face shining with sweat, his breath coming in hoarse gasps. They lay close together, hand in hand, and so Iain found them when he too reached the path and paused to regain his breath.

There was no time to linger. It was almost dark, the shadows increasing between the trees. Iain was soon on his feet again, urging Nick to stand and, supported by them both, to walk along the path.

It was just wide enough for the three of them, close together, entwined like lovers. Nick hung between Iain and Tracy, his arms across their shoulders, one foot dragging. They went slowly and Tracy saw with thankfulness the red and white 'bulls-eye' mark on tree and rocks which betokened the real, waymarked path. She sighed with relief. However far they must go now, and even though they must apparently spend the night somewhere on the mountain, she knew with a quiet certainty that they would reach the bottom. To all intents and purposes, they were safe. However uncomfortable the next few hours would be, they were safe. Life would go on for her, as for a time she had feared that it would not.

Iain was speaking and she brought her attention back to the present.

'Just a bit further,' he was saying encouragingly. 'I passed it on the way up – a kind of shelter, like a small ridge tent, made of large strips of bark slung across a couple of poles. It'll be draughty – but better than a night in the open. It's cold at night – ah, there it is!'

Tracy peered through the gloom. There, just ahead of them on the path, was the hut that Iain had described. A woodman's shelter, she supposed; scarcely large enough for the three of them, but welcome enough nevertheless. They stopped at its entrance and Nick sank to the ground.

'Whew – thank goodness! That wasn't pleasant.' He glanced up at them both. 'Seems I owe you an apology, Iain.'

'Forget it – we've got other things to think of now.' Iain glanced at Tracy. 'Wood first for a fire – and enough to keep us going all night! But we'll have to be quick; it's almost dark now and I don't want you wandering along that path and getting lost again.' His voice softened as he said, almost under his breath, 'I can't afford to lose you again.'

It was fully dark by the time they felt that all that could be done was complete. Nick was in the tent, his injured ankle bound with wadding and bandages from Iain's rucksack, his back propped against the stout pole at the back. Tracy and Iain had col-

213

lected a huge pile of wood – fallen branches, pine cones, twigs – which was now massed at the entrance. The fire had been lit a few feet away– 'We can't risk sparks on the roof!' Iain had said with a grim smile – and he was now busy with a small pan, stirring something that smelled savoury and appetising. Tracy realised with a jolt how hungry she was; except for a few pieces of chocolate, she and Nick had eaten nothing for over seven hours.

'I don't understand,' she said, watching Iain; the shadows had deepened in the firelight. 'How did you find us? How did you know where to look? And why have you got all these things with you – bandages, food, a saucepan even? You didn't take them up the mountain with you.'

'No. But when you left, I thought perhaps you'd had second thoughts about trying to walk down the mountain. I couldn't believe you would be so foolish – so reckless.' His voice shook a little, but whether with anger or some other emotion, Tracy was unsure. He went on, 'I finished my coffee and sat for a while chatting to the woman in the chalet. She told me that the path was impassable. I went back to the cable-car after a while, saw no sign of you, and decided you must have already gone down.'

'You went down yourself?'

'Yes, and when I reached the bottom I met the Marchants – the couple you were with yesterday.' Tracy wanted to ask how he knew that, but remained silent. 'They told me they'd been there for nearly an hour, just sitting and watching the cable-car, looking at the lake and so on as they had their lunch. They said they hadn't seen you come down. And when I asked in the booking office, the man there said you had not returned. I knew then that you *had* taken the path down the mountain.'

'But I still don't see–'

'I went back up, to see if you'd given up – but there was no sign. So I started down the path myself. I could follow your footprints part of the way, along the edge of the snow. Then I lost them – you must have gone through the trees, where there was no snow to betray you.'

'It was patchy in places,' Tracy said, remembering. 'We kept thinking we'd got to the end of it, and then there was more ahead. And every time we turned a little, to work round the edge, we must have got further from the path…' Her voice trembled and broke, and Iain moved quickly across to

215

her, his arm round her shoulders, pressing her against him.

'It's all over now... Well, I could see that I had little chance of finding you that way. It would have been crazy for me to get lost too – no one would have known where to look for any of us! And the weather was getting worse. It was just then that the thunderstorm broke.' He was quiet for a moment. 'The thought of you – out there on that hillside, with thunder and lightning crashing round you – I tell you, Tracy, I nearly went mad.'

'What did you do then?' Tracy's voice was small. She too was recalling the horror of that storm.

'Well, I thought the best thing was to get down to the bottom again, call out a search party. So back I went in the cable-car. But it took too long; too long to explain; too long to convince the right people that you were up there, in danger. They all thought that you must have gone back, taken shelter in one of the chalets or something... Eventually, I lost patience. I knew that if you weren't found before dark you'd be in real trouble. I packed some food and first-aid equipment and set off myself, coming up the waymarked path from the bottom. They clear it, you see, as the snow melts, so I was able to make quite good speed. I left a message for Melissa and she'll get a party organised first thing in the morning – at first light.'

Tracy nodded. She had forgotten Melissa, but now she remembered – remembered the way Iain had greeted the beautiful courier on the first morning, the way they'd been together almost ever since; she remembered the two of them coming out of the village house, talking to the old woman; the white sports car on the mountain track yesterday.

And suddenly, in spite of the fire, she was cold. She drew away from Iain's arms and said quickly, 'The food – is it ready yet? I'm starving!'

Immediately, Iain was all concern for her. He poured hot soup into three bowls, crawled into the tent to rouse Nick, who had been dozing, and set a pan of water on the fire. Tracy, her appetite gone, took her bowl and ate listlessly; and then felt fresh hunger and spooned the soup greedily.

'And now,' Iain said when they had finished off with rolls and steaming coffee. 'It's time you got some sleep. You must be exhausted.' He settled Nick, who had dozed again as soon as he had finished eating, and said to Tracy, 'I think he'll be feeling a lot better tomorrow. It's not a break – just a sprain. Put paid to the rest of his walking holiday, though, I'm afraid!'

'Poor Nick,' Tracy said, looking down at him as he slept. 'He didn't mean to cause so much trouble.'

'Few people ever do,' Iain reached out and drew her to him. 'Tell me, Tracy – this engagement of yours–'

'It's off. It was never really on – I realised that. Everything seemed such a muddle.' She swayed slightly and Iain's arms tightened around her.

'You're dead tired,' he said, his eyes almost black in the leaping firelight. 'Go to sleep now, Tracy. I'll keep an eye on the fire. And don't worry – about anything. It's going to be all right.' He laid her down at the edge of the hut, just inside and close to Nick. Then he covered her with a thin, warm blanket from his rucksack. For a moment he bent over her, his eyes on her face, and then, as Tracy's heavy lids drooped, she was aware of gentle lips brushing her cheek...

She slept then, but woke several times in the night. And each time she woke, she could see silhouetted against the glowing embers of the fire, Iain's powerful body and strong profile. And once, pale in the clear sky, she saw over his shoulder the broad crescent of the rising moon.

ELEVEN

Somewhere outside, a cuckoo was calling. It called insistently – like an alarm-clock, intent on waking her. A soft breeze touched Tracy's face and she stirred, turned over and was suddenly awake.

For a few moments she lay bewildered, staring at the ceiling. Her mind was a confused memory of treacherous paths, a slope too steep to cross, paths too narrow to walk on, jumbled rocks, cliffs, fallen trees, a smooth fall of frozen snow sweeping its way to the lake thousands of feet below. A cold memory of panic flooded her as she thought of Nick's accident, her own feeling of helplessness as she realised that their lives now depended on her; that somehow, alone, she had to get down the mountain, fetch help, lead the rescuers back to Nick. And then – relaxing suddenly in the comfortable bed, she recalled her relief as she realised that Iain was there, that they would, after all, be safe.

But her memories of Iain, too, were confused. He had looked at her with love, held her in his arms. He had cared for her and for Nick, found them shelter, fed them and watched over them during the night. He had come specially to search for them, and Tracy had gone to sleep beside him on the mountain, warmed by his gentle kiss, feeling a security that she had not known for years.

Yet, when she had woken this morning, feeling the cool morning air on her cheek, opening her eyes to the pale dawn filtering through the trees, she had known a moment's chilling doubt. In that moment, she had looked for Iain and found him gone; and as she sat up, suddenly anxious, she remembered Melissa.

Melissa! How could she have forgotten the beautiful courier, the cool, competent auburn-haired girl who coped with everything so admirably, who would never have got lost on a mountain, who was invariably well-groomed – Tracy glanced down at her own dishevelled person and winced – and who had greeted Iain with such disturbing intimacy? How could she have forgotten the house in the village where both seemed to be honoured guests; the glimpse of the white sports car high on the mountains, the flash of kingfisher blue amongst the trees – *and that's how he knew we were with the Marchants,* Tracy thought suddenly. *He was there too, and saw us!*

She lay down again, bewildered. What did it all mean? Ever since she had arrived in Yugoslavia – no, earlier than that, from the moment she had seen him at the airport in London – Tracy had been disturbingly aware of Iain Macalister. She had fought the awareness, afraid to admit her own growing love even to herself, afraid of the hurt of loving a man who seemed to despise her. And then, in the end, it had been too much for her; and she had been forced to acknowledge it. And last night it had seemed, to her joy, that her love was, after all, returned. She had gone to sleep in the certainty that Iain loved her as she loved him.

It must have been a dream, an illusion. Naturally Iain, just as any man would have been had been relieved to find them relatively safe. Naturally, finding her exhausted and frightened, Nick injured and helpless, he had been gentle and considerate with them both. Anything more than that must be in her own imagination. Tracy's cheeks burned as she recalled the way she had clung to him, her broken whispers. He must have been embarrassed as she now felt – no doubt that was why he had disappeared now. He must be wondering how she would behave this morning, whether she would act possessively, hinting that there had been something more than relief and comradeship between them...

Well, she would soon put his mind at rest! There must be no more moments of intimacy, no more running to his arms for comfort. She and Nick had been foolish; Iain had rescued them. Proper gratitude was called for – but nothing more.

A crackling of twigs told her that Iain was returning along the path, and she hastily scrambled up and was trying to tidy herself when he appeared. He saw her and stopped; for a moment they looked at each other in the pale light of the mountain morning, and then Tracy turned away, brushing at her clothes.

'I was just trying to make myself look presentable!' She heard her voice, light and brittle. 'Nick's still asleep. What time is it?'

'Half-past three.' He came to her side,

looking down at her.

'You must be utterly tired of us!' she exclaimed, turning away to look down through the trees, trying to catch a glimpse of the valley below. 'We've been nothing but trouble to you.'

'I wouldn't say that.' He was watching her, his face shuttered and withdrawn, a strange expression in his eyes. 'I was very glad to find you safe.'

Tracy turned and met his eyes. She hoped that hers betrayed none of her real feelings; she was determined to spare him further embarrassment. She held out her hand and said simply, 'I really am very grateful Mr Macalister. I was very frightened last night, before you came.'

He took the small hand in his, gazing at the slim white fingers that lay in his brown palm.

'Last night, you called me Iain.'

Tracy hesitated. She wanted, desperately to use his name; but she was afraid that if she did so, he would hear the love in her voice, that he would recognise her feelings and either be totally embarrassed or which might be worse – dismiss it as a mere reaction from yesterday's events.

He glanced at her, his blue eyes dark. And

then, to her inexpressible relief, she heard a faint call – the sound of voices somewhere below them – the shrill of a whistle.

'The search party!' he exclaimed, dropping her hand. He pulled his own whistle from his pocket and blew several blasts on it. 'That will have awakened young Nick! We'll soon be down, Tracy.' And then he turned back to her, caught her hand again and gave her a long look. 'And then, when everything's over, I'll want to see you again. We've got some talking to do, you and I.'

Tracy turned over again in bed, gazing out through the gauzy curtains to the shadowy mountains beyond. What could Iain want to talk to her about? The dangers of exploring mountains when you were ill-equipped, when you didn't know the way and had been warned of the dangers? The foolishness of trusting to strange young men who professed to be climbers but had obviously had no experience of conditions like these? Or the stupidity of falling in love on holiday – of throwing oneself at every attractive man in sight, regardless of whether he was already attached or not?

There was nothing else, Tracy was sure, that Iain could want to say to her, and she hoped fervently that he had forgotten his words. Certainly he had not referred to them again on that journey down the mountain when, moving slowly ahead of the stretcher that had been brought, they descended the twisting path through the trees. There had been little opportunity for intimate talk, with the tall Yugoslavians so close behind, and Nick making rather contrived but cheerful conversation from his helpless position. Tracy, painfully aware of the trouble they had caused, had been unable to think of a thing to say, while Iain had been more withdrawn than ever, his eyes hooded. Only his hand, clasping Tracy's every now and then to help her over a fallen tree or past a tricky outcrop of rock, was as warm and steady as before.

At the bottom of the mountain, when at last they came along the last stretch of woodland path and found themselves once more blessedly on the road, they had found a large car waiting for them; and in it, immaculate as ever although it was still only six-o'clock, was Melissa.

The relief of being at last off the mountain, her feet once again on a road, swept over Tracy and she swayed suddenly. She found herself supported by strong arms –

whose, she never knew – and lifted into the car. Ridiculous tears flooded her eyes, spilling down her cheeks, and she was aware of Iain's concerned face, of Melissa's re-assuring smile.

'It's just reaction,' she was saying. 'You've had a rotten time. Cry if you like – cry it away.' And Tracy, past all shame now, leant her head against the side of the car, accepted the handkerchief that Melissa gave her, and wept as if her heart was broken.

And perhaps it had been, she thought now as she lay in bed several hours later. A hot bath, breakfast and a long sleep in bed had been just what she needed; she felt calm now, and rested. But she was sadly aware that it had not only been reaction from shock that had caused her tears at the foot of the mountain; it had been her own private admission, on seeing Melissa, that Iain was not for her; that she must give up all thoughts of winning his love, that she must say goodbye to him next week, when the holiday ended, and go back to her cottage in Herefordshire, take up the threads of her old life again – those that were left – and forget him.

But she knew that she could never do that; that the memory of being held in his arms, brushed by his lips, would stay with her for ever; a treasure locked in her heart for always.

A light tap on the bedroom door roused her from her thoughts. She sat up, frowning, puzzled. The tap came again, and with it a deep, familiar voice that brought the blood to her cheeks.

'Tracy! Are you awake, lassie?'

'Yes.' Her voice was weak, scared. Why was he here?

'I've brought you some coffee. May I bring it in?'

He was in before she could reply, his eyes piercing under the dark brows. Tracy shrank back, pulling the bedclothes to her chin, and his mouth widened in a smile.

'It's all right, I have no ulterior motive. Or just one, anyway.' He placed the tray beside her bed. 'Drink this, now, and then get up. I'll see you outside in – we'll say twenty minutes, shall we?' His hand rested lightly on her hair, ruffling the short curls. 'Don't look so frightened, lassie – I'll not hurt you! But we need to talk, you and I, and I'll not wait much longer! Twenty minutes.'

He was gone; and Tracy sat up, drinking her coffee thoughtfully. What he should have to say, she had no idea; but it had been plain from his manner that he was determined to say it. She would simply have to grit her teeth and listen.

And then, if possible, she would keep well out of his way for the last few days of the holiday. To see him, talk to him, could only be pain; and Tracy had had enough of pain.

She got out of bed and dressed slowly, putting on a plain yellow frock with a small roll-collar that set off her slim figure and small, well-shaped head to perfection. She brushed the pale gold curls till they shone, noticed with satisfaction that the wide green eyes looked clear and fresh from her long sleep, and slipped her feet into sandals.

How long had she slept? She glanced at her watch and discovered with surprise that it was almost five – she had slept for eight hours! She wondered how Nick was now, and whether he was worried about her – not that there was any reason to be – and made up her mind to go and see him at once.

But she had not reckoned with Iain Macalister. As she came down the stairs, he was waiting at the bottom. He glanced up, gave her a smile of admiration and came forward.

'I thought I'd just go and see Nick–'

'No need. I've just been. He's fine now,

the doctor's seen his ankle and says a few days' rest is all that's needed. And Marela had taken him some coffee. I think you'll find he's quite all right.' She remembered Nick's friendship with the pretty receptionist and, catching Iain's eye, smiled. 'So we can be going about our business,' he went on, giving her hand a gentle squeeze. 'Come on.'

Tracy followed him outside and saw, with surprise and misgiving, that Melissa's white sports car stood outside. Iain walked over to it, opened the passenger door and gently pushed her in. Then he went round to the driver's seat and took his place. Tracy stared at him, bewildered.

'We're going to see someone,' he said, smiling at her puzzled frown. 'And on the way I am going to tell you a story. I think you need to know something about me, Tracy.'

Iain started the car and let in the clutch. The white car moved smoothly away down the slope, through the woods. They reached the lake and Iain turned the car, running alongside the scarcely-rippling waters. Around them the mountains reared and Tracy could not repress a shiver as she gazed up at the dark conifers and the snow, remembering the terrible journey down yesterday – was it only yesterday? And then they were passing between the great walls of rocks, running out of the valley and climbing slowly towards the jagged white peaks of the Triglav range. They passed other valleys, smaller lakes, high mountain villages; and at last, drawing off the road so that they could look down into a deep valley, thick with trees and with a green, white-flecked stream far below, Iain stopped the car. He turned and looked deep into Tracy's eyes, and as she looked back her heart seemed to pause in its beating before it began to race.

'Tracy,' Iain said, and his voice was very deep. 'You know why I've brought you here, don't you?'

Wordlessly, she shook her head. He reached for her, taking her in his arms, drawing her close. He brushed his lips gently down the curve of her cheek, turning her face with his cupped hand, kissed the corners of her mouth, her throat, her ears, her eyes, then, finally, her mouth again.

'You do know, my little lass, my little mountain lass,' he murmured huskily, and kissed her again and again, until she was breathless, her mouth answering his, her arms tight about his neck. Her heart beat against his, her pulses raced with his, her mind was dizzy with their kissing; and when at last he released her lips she lay against him, dazed and exhausted by the sweet wildness of their emotion.

'Don't tell me now you don't know,' he whispered again, his hand in her hair. 'Don't tell me you don't know that I love you – that we belong together – and that from now on nothing – *nothing*, you understand – is going to come between us!'

'But, Iain–' the words were forced from her, '–what about Melissa?'

'Melissa?' His tone was genuinely puzzled and she raised her face to stare at him.

'Yes – Melissa. This is her car. You're – Iain, I thought you loved Melissa!'

'Well, of course I do!' he answered astonished. And then, with a sudden shout of laughter. 'Of course I do, you silly little, darling little mountain goat! Melissa's my cousin! We were brought up together.'

'Your – cousin?'

'Aye – and that's all! We were brought up as brother and sister.' He smiled down at her. 'I can see I shall have to tell you my whole family history! But first–' suiting the action to the words, '–I must just kiss away that pretty little frown on your forehead.

There! Now, are you sitting comfortably?'

Tracy snuggled down in his arms. There was obviously a good deal yet to know about Iain Macalister – but the fact that Melissa was his cousin was the most important. She could listen to the rest with no fears.

'This story goes back to just before the war,' Iain began, his eyes on the distant mountains. 'Long before you were born, my wee mountain lassie. Before I was born, too. It begins with my father.'

'Your father?'

'Aye. He was a great engineer, my father, running his own business at home in Edinburgh and with ideas for expanding. Not just over Scotland, or England either, but into Europe. He had advanced ideas. He came to Europe on a tour, looking out for new methods, new ideas but also for work that he could do – a way to get his foot in the door. He was determined to build up his wee business into something really big.

'So he came to Yugoslavia – to Slovenia. And while he was here he met and fell in love with a local girl; a very beautiful girl. And she fell in love with him.'

'And–?'

'And so, of course, they wanted to get married. But her parents were very much

232

against the idea. They didn't approve at all of their daughter marrying a poor Scots engineer. And nothing would make them change their minds. So, one day, my father came for her – and they ran away together. They went back to Scotland, and they got married.'

'And she was your mother?' Tracy pictured the beautiful young Slovenian girl, the elopement across Europe, the arrival in Scotland. How strange it must all have been; and how romantic!

'Aye, she was my mother. She taught me her language, told me of her people, and her country. But before that – when she had only been in Scotland for a short while – the war came. There could be no communication with her parents, with any of her family. It was a great distress to her, for she never knew whether they had forgiven her for running away. She longed to know how they were – whether they were in danger, and as time went on, whether they were even still alive. But there was no word.'

'And after the war? Couldn't she find out then?'

'After the war, my father became ill. He developed a terrible wasting disease, which went on for years, growing a little worse all the time. My mother could not leave him. She had to look after him as well as myself and Melissa, whose parents were both killed in an accident. And as I grew up, I studied hard, took my engineering degree and took over the business. My father managed to keep the reins in his hands until I could take over; but it was a great effort for him.'

'It was dreadful for you all.' Tracy spoke with complete understanding. 'My own father was ill for a long time.' Iain glanced at her and took her hand, caressing the fingers gently. She knew that they were both thinking of his remarks made in the valley of the gorge – his cutting accusations about sickrooms: and she said gently, 'We both understand now – don't we? Go on with your story.'

'My father died last year,' he continued, his voice low. 'It had always been a dream of my mother's that one day she would come back – return to Slovenia and find her family. But by this time, she was afraid – afraid that they might have gone, might have died or – perhaps worse than anything – not welcomed her. Last year, Melissa came here as a courier. She tried to find my grandparents; but there was no trace of them.'

His eyes stared unseeingly out over the

valley. The shadows were lengthening as the sun sank behind the mountains. In the distance, the snowy peaks were tinged with pink. Tracy thought again of the Slovenian woman, living for years in a foreign land, not knowing what had happened to her parents, whether they lived or died; and she blinked away tears.

'This year, I felt that the business was steady enough for me to leave it. I had promised my mother that I would go as soon as I could to find out what had happened to them. Melissa had been in London all winter, but she came out a few weeks ago to begin arranging the holidays for this year – and she sent word that she thought she had discovered something. I booked immediately – luckily, as this is the first holiday of the season, there were still one or two vacancies. I came out and Melissa took me to see an old woman in Belanice.' He paused and looked down at Tracy, his eyes shining as blue as the sky beyond. 'The old woman was my mother's aunt. And two days ago, after many family talks – for the grandparents are old now, and the news had to be broken gently – Melissa and I went up into the mountains. We went to a hut high in the forest near the foot of Triglav; and there we found my grandparents!'

'I saw the car there,' Tracy said quietly. 'I thought I saw Melissa – and you.'

'And I saw you. I saw your dear little sprite's face in the window going past. And I was consumed with a fire of jealousy, even in the midst of my happiness, because you were with young Lester and I wanted you so much for myself.'

'Even then?' she said in wonder. 'Did you – love me – even then?'

'Then and before then! I loved you from the moment you spilt coffee on me at the airport, and blamed me for my own misfortune! I loved you when I tried to offer an olive branch at the hotel, and at Lipice, and you threw my olive branch back in my face! I loved you when we sat together watching those beautiful horses and I knew that you felt just as I did about them. I loved you more and more every time I saw you. When we were in the gorge, I felt sure that you loved me too – and when you spurned me, told me you were engaged to Lester and left me there, I felt I could throw myself into that turbulent water. You drove me mad, with your little sprite's face, your green eyes and your prickly ways. You came between me and my sleep – between me and my search for a family.' He stopped and drew her close against his heart, his arms like steel round her body. 'And when I thought I'd lost you on that damned mountain – Tracy, don't you ever do such a thing again. There isn't a man made who could stand such agony twice!'

Tracy said, shakily. 'I didn't mean to – I never really wanted to walk down. I was afraid from the first moment.'

'Never mind. It's over now.' His lips found hers. 'But for us – this is just a beginning. How soon – how soon can you marry me, Tracy?'

'As soon as you like,' she said softly.

And then, after a pause which was eminently satisfactory on both sides, he said, 'So I too will find my happiness in Slovenia, just as my parents did before me. And now, my darling sprite of the mountains, I am taking you to meet my grandparents. They were happy the other day, when they met me for the first time and knew that their daughter was well and had had a happy life – for in spite of my father's illness, they *were* happy – and to meet you, to know that we too love Slovenia and our children will too; that will complete their joy. And then–' his arm tightened about her,

'–it will be home for us; home to a wedding and our own happiness. Oh, Tracy...' And, his lips brushing hers again, he began to murmur softly, words and endearments that she scarcely understood but which yet sounded beautifully familiar and right.

The sky had darkened to a rich, deep blue, and the mountains glowed with the last apricot rays of sunlight. And Tracy, lifting her face for a moment from Iain's shoulder, saw just rising in a deep rift in the mountains, the pale yellow crescent of the moon; with, quite close to it, a single brilliant star.

The publishers hope that this book has given you enjoyable reading. Large Print Books are especially designed to be as easy to see and hold as possible. If you wish a complete list of our books please ask at your local library or write directly to:

Dales Large Print Books
Magna House, Long Preston,
Skipton, North Yorkshire.
BD23 4ND

This Large Print Book for the partially sighted, who cannot read normal print, is published under the auspices of

THE ULVERSCROFT FOUNDATION

THE ULVERSCROFT FOUNDATION

... we hope that you have enjoyed this Large Print Book. Please think for a moment about those people who have worse eyesight problems than you ... and are unable to even read or enjoy Large Print, without great difficulty.

You can help them by sending a donation, large or small to:

**The Ulverscroft Foundation,
1, The Green, Bradgate Road,
Anstey, Leicestershire, LE7 7FU,
England.**
or request a copy of our brochure for more details.

The Foundation will use all your help to assist those people who are handicapped by various sight problems and need special attention.

Thank you very much for your help.